Lost Without You

M. O'KEEFE

Dear Reader!

I am so excited about this new series – The Debt. I've had this idea about five teenagers owing a powerful and dangerous man a debt and not knowing when or how they were going to have to repay it. It's a series about friendship and the lengths people will go for love and redemption. Basically, it's all my favorite things.

And I hope it's yours, too!

THE DEBT: A PROLOGUE (free)
LOST WITHOUT YOU (includes The Debt)
WHERE I BELONG

If you read THE DEBT: A PROLOGUE skip ahead to PART 2!

PART I

1

Cedar Ridge High School
San Francisco, CA
Beth

KISSING TOMMY MACNEILL was like eating a bag of Skittles. Magic Skittles.

Because he was sweet, yes. So sweet. But the magic part was that kissing him made me sweet, too. Every time his lips touched mine, we got sweeter together.

We were delicious.

I can be honest—I was obsessed with kissing Tommy MacNeill.

"Beth," he said as I led him towards the art room at school. The art room was deserted at lunch and it was where we made out. The art room was pretty much the best place in the world. "We can't keep doing this."

"But we can." I grinned at him over my shoulder and his hand twitched in mine and I knew he was excited.

Because Tommy—stoic, silent Tommy—had a tell.

The tips of his ears glowed red when he was excited. Or embarrassed.

But he wasn't embarrassed right now—oh no, these were his excited ears.

LOTS of people could know this about Tommy—they only had to spend five minutes with him and it was obvious. But Tommy didn't spend a whole lot of time with anyone that wasn't from St. Jude's Home for Court-Placed Juveniles.

And really—these days—he only spent time with me.

And really—these days—I only spent time with him.

Because of the Skittles, and his ears, and the way his hands on my body made me feel warm and cold and light and heavy all at once. Tommy didn't say much—I did most of the talking—but he listened. I mean…really listened. And maybe that wasn't a big deal to the rest of the world.

But I'd never been listened to. Not once. Not even a little.

And this was the shittiest time in my life, by like a mile, but it was also the best.

Because of Tommy.

The art room door closed behind us, shutting us in its turpentine-scented hush, and he put his hands on my waist, turning me so I faced him.

"Ahhh," I said, getting a good look at his face, "not so eager to stop now, are you, Tommy?"

Silent, with his glowing ears and his white-hot eyes, he walked us back into the corner where we spent most of our lunch hour. The past few days we didn't even have our lunch first, we just came right here. And part of me felt guilty because Tommy needed to eat.

Like for real.

Tommy was tall, but he was so thin. When his shirt pushed up against his back in the wind, I could see the outline of his ribs against his skin. And his skin was always dry, like he was parched on the inside. Every day when he got to school, he stood at the drinking fountain for like ten minutes, sucking down water. Filling himself up.

It broke my heart.

I wasn't sure why The Pastor and His Wife didn't feed Tommy like they should. They had to give him lunch when he went to school, and most of us from the home gave him part of our lunches too. But at St. Joke's (we called St. Jude's St. Joke's, which wasn't funny, but it's what we had) they barely gave him anything. Made him sit at the table without a plate while we had a regular dinner—a gross one, but still.

Tommy said it was punishment, but when I asked him what he was being punished for he didn't have an answer.

And it was only one of the many crazy things that went on in our foster home.

But the way Tommy was looking at me right now, his blue eyes hot and his lids all heavy…who needed food when we had this thing between us? This art-room thing?

"Someday we're going to get caught," he said, and my back hit the corkboard wall.

"I don't care," I whispered because I was breathless and my heart was beating funny.

He touched my hair, the big wild poof of it, held in place by a ponytail holder. He kept asking me to take it down, but my hair was a *situation*. And putting it back up was a *process*.

No time for situations or processes when we had kissing to do.

I grinned at him. And he grinned at me, but his grin…it didn't have any joy in it. He was nervous, and I didn't want to be nervous. We had hours of nervous back at St. Joke's. Looking over our shoulders and being as small as we could be and still survive.

Here at school, here with him—this was where we were happy. This was where we were ourselves. And speaking for myself, I was more me here than I'd ever been in my life.

I was me squared. Me times a thousand.

I used my fingers to push his lips around, to lift the

sides a little higher like that might give him some joy. "Smile," I said. "For real."

I crossed my eyes at him and finally he laughed, the breathy *harrumph* of a laugh that made me happy. He pretended to bite me and I pulled my hands from his lips to his hair. The thick white buzz cut felt like an old-fashioned brush against my fingers. Back and forth I rubbed it, smooth and bristly in turns.

"Do you look like your mom or your dad?" I asked. I was a little obsessed with this. With the way we looked like other people in our families. Because I didn't look like anyone in my family. My mom was black and my dad was white and I had the red hair and freckles that came from a mutation in the MC1R gene.

I was an anomaly in my family. In a whole bunch of ways.

And that wasn't as fun as it sounds.

But Tommy, he looked like a Viking or something. Like his size (big) and his eyes (blue) and his hair (white) had been passed down from hundreds of years ago. There'd been some kind of fur-covered dude, in the bow of a boat, sailing around the North Sea who looked just like Tommy.

Is it obvious I've spent a lot of time thinking about this?

"I never met my dad," he said, closing his eyes and letting me pet him. He liked this. He really liked this.

So I put both hands on the job, using my nails a little, and he groaned in his throat. I never met my dad either. He'd been a donor in a sperm bank when my mom was forty and decided she needed to have a kid. "Barely remember my mom."

"What about your grandparents?"

His eyes flew open, his blue eyes so startling every time. Like at night when we got locked into our separate rooms at St. Joke's, I'd think, *there's no way his eyes are that blue. No eyes are that blue.* And then in the morning when The Pastor let us out, there was Tommy in the hallway, with his blue, blue eyes.

"Why are you talking about this?" he asked.

"Because we never have before."

"I have a grandfather. He's like a lemon farmer or something near Santa Barbara. When I got put in the system he filed paperwork relinquishing all rights."

"He…gave you up?"

"Without even meeting me."

"I'm sorry." I'm not sure how I kept getting surprised by how shitty people could be. I'd been at St. Jude's for three months and I thought I'd heard it all, every awful thing that an adult could do to a kid.

But there was always more. Endless, heartbreaking more.

He shrugged like it was no big deal. "What about your mom?" he asked.

"You really want to talk about this?"

"You started it," he said with a genuine laugh. "And you never talk about your mom. I don't even know how you ended up at St. Joke's."

"Because it's boring and dumb." I lifted his hand and looked at his watch, because the last thing I wanted was to talk about my mom and how I ended up in our court-placed foster home. "We've only got fifteen minutes of lunch left."

"I wish…" he said and I almost stopped him. Kids like us…we had no business wishing anything. I learned that a long time ago. Simon, Tommy's roommate—that guy wished. He wished and he wished and it got him nowhere.

But Tommy never told me what he wished, and I knew I was part of whatever it was. Just like he was part of all my wishes that I could never say out loud.

"I wish we were five years older," he said. "And I could take you to a movie or something, and we could…we could just be normal."

"I wish we were five years older and we didn't have to make out in the high school art room."

"I wish you'd take down your hair."

"I wish you'd take down your pants."

His mouth fell open, my so easily shocked Tommy. And I laughed, wiping my hands over his face, closing his mouth.

My mother would die if she knew I was doing this. In fact my mother had done everything she could to make sure I'd *never* do this. She'd tried to make me scared and answered questions about my body with clinical doctor answers that didn't answer anything at all.

She wanted me to believe that girls who liked the kind of stuff we did in the art room—those girls were bad.

But my body knew she was wrong. There was nothing bad about what me and Tommy did in the art room.

"I like what we do here," I whispered.

"Me too." His lips moved beneath my fingers and I felt the simmering, waiting tension in my body.

"Remember?" I swallowed, an audible gulp. I could feel myself blushing and I stared down at the chipped red Formica of the countertop next to us. "What you did last time?"

Against my stomach, he was hard. And where he was hard, I was soft and that felt like the best thing in the world.

"Oh, I remember," he said. "I think I'll remember for the rest of my life."

"I want to do it for you," I said, finally brave enough to lift my eyes to his face. "I want to make you come."

He shook his head. "No."

"Why?"

"Because we're in an art room at lunch, Beth. Because someone could walk in any minute… Fuck," he breathed. No one in all my sixteen years swore around me, and I loved it when he did it. I loved how real it was. And how every time he swore it was like the word came up from his belly. He swore like he meant it. It was dirty.

And I was really beginning to love *dirty*.

He kissed me. Hot and sweet and more exciting than I knew what to do with. It hurt between my legs, not like an ouch hurt. But…you know, an ache. And I could feel how wet I was. I would feel how wet I was for the rest of the day, and I wasn't sure if that was gross or not. Seemed like it might be? Like were my panties supposed to be…so wet?

But last time, when he put his hand under my skirt and felt how wet I was…he said I was perfect.

His tongue touched mine and I stopped worrying about anything. I could barely think. His chest pushed up against me and I moaned low in my throat because he felt so good like that.

And this was fun. And Skittley-delicious. But I knew there was more than kissing and pushing up against each other. Last time showed me there was *so much more*.

So I reached for him again, my hand to the front of his jeans, and I got the impression of him beneath the denim. Really big. Too big? I wondered. Was that a thing? Not for us, I decided.

We, when we finally had sex, we would be perfect.

And I could not wait. I imagined us in a hotel room. Crisp white sheets that didn't smell like bleach. Sunlight and all the time in the world.

And no fear. Not ever again.

I squeezed him through his pants, pressed the heel of my palm against the top of his dick. God, even thinking that word was exciting.

He grabbed my hand, slapped my palm down on the counter beside us. And held me there. "You gotta stop that," he said. "For real."

I tried to pull away but he wouldn't let me. And oh, God…oh God, I liked that. I really liked that. I mean, it's not like I thought he meant it. He wasn't really going to hurt me. Or hold me there against my will. Not Tommy.

It was just…exciting. Like…so exciting. Because I felt so safe with him. I'd never felt so safe with anyone in my life. If I said stop, he'd stop. If I said no, he'd let me go. If I said yes, well…

Rosa, my roommate at St. Joke's, was pregnant. Sixteen and pregnant. And the way she talked about her boyfriend I knew they had this thing going between them.

Lust and like and trust and probably love, all mixed up into one big, wild, out-of-control feeling. And it was bad, what was happening to her, being pregnant and at St. Joke's. But she told me all the time that she was lucky, too.

Because she knew what real love was.

And that was a really lucky thing.

It was weird to feel lucky in all this shit we were in…but there you go.

Tommy's breath was hot against my face. His free hand—the one that wasn't holding my hand down—burned through my shirt right to my skin. He shifted and his knee pressed against me *there* and I saw sparks. Real sparks behind my closed eyes, and they were coming from between my legs. Like embers off a fire.

I pulled him against me, opening my legs so his knee went between them.

His knee…his hand holding me down. I felt *it* happening in my body. Like last time. I pulled back, looking at Tommy. Were we supposed to talk about this? I wanted to. I wanted to tell him what I needed. What I felt.

"Like that?" he whispered, pushing up higher against me.

I nodded, gulping air.

That look on his face, in his blue eyes…the way he

stared at me, watching me. Oh, God, he knew. He knew what he was doing. He knew what I wanted. With the hand he wasn't holding down, I reached for him—grabbed onto him like I was in a storm-tossed ocean and he was a piece of wood floating by to save me.

My fingers slipped up under his shirt, to the smooth skin of his sides. And he twitched away from me and I wasn't sure if it was because of his ribs or the old scars that crisscrossed his back.

The Pastor did that, too. Put those scars on him.

For a second, I stilled. The weight of everything, the *awfulness* of how we lived was too much.

"Hey," he said, leaning away from me, "you want to stop?"

"No." I shook my head.

"You went someplace else there for a second."

"No. I'm here. With you. I'm always here with you."

He kissed me again, soft and sweet.

"Spread your legs wider," he said and I did. I would do anything he asked. I was lost in him.

"Students!"

Tommy jerked away from me so fast, he bumped into the counter and sent a bunch of student perspective drawings crashing to the floor. He bent and picked them up, probably trying to hide his boner, and I stood, petrified, staring at Mr. Abrahams.

The principal.

My body dried up in heartbeat. That thorny exciting feeling between my legs vanished. Leaving only fear.

We've been caught.

"Mr. Abrahams," I said, trying to make my voice steady. Trying to make my whole body steady, but this was serious.

And this was bad.

"I can explain," I said. My voice was too high and I laughed nervously. My mother would tell me that I was broadcasting my insecurities and that no one would take me seriously this way.

She was probably right.

He lifted one side of his unibrow. "Oh, I think it's clear what you were doing."

"But—"

He lifted his hand, and I shut my mouth.

"I have to say, Ms. Renshaw." God, I hated when he called me by my last name. It made me feel even more guilty. Mr. Abrahams wasn't a bad guy, he just didn't seem to know how ineffective he was. "This behavior is not at all what I expect from you. Your transcripts when you transferred here were exemplary. Honor roll grades. Student Council. Choir. Theater. But in your three months at Cedar High, you just don't seem to care."

I don't, I wanted to shout. *Caring gets you nowhere! It gives you ulcers and makes your hair fall out and your mother just abandons you anyway, so why care?*

But I didn't say any of that.

Mr. Abrahams's eyes shifted over Tommy like he didn't even deserve a lecture. This kind of thing was what people expected from him. And that wasn't fair either. Because Tommy cared more than I did. Tommy cared more than anyone I knew.

"It's my fault," Tommy said as if he knew the line he was supposed to say. "I convinced her to come here."

"Is that true?" Abrahams asked, going on full alert like a sexual assault hound dog.

"No," I said very evenly and clearly. "I am here because I want to be here."

There was a loaded moment while Abrahams decided whether or not to believe me.

"Just clear out of the art room." Mr. Abrahams sighed like we were just so disappointing.

Tommy, having put the artwork back on the counter, looked at me, eyes wide. And I knew what he was thinking—*is that it? No punishment? No telling The Pastor?* I started to smile, relief making me dizzy. Tommy grabbed my hand and began to pull me out of the corner, like he was saving me from a fire. And maybe he was, because if The Pastor found out about us being together, it would be bad for everyone at St. Joke's.

He'd punish all of us.

"Tommy," Mr. Abrahams said as we got to the door. "This is against the conditions of your court placement. You know I have to notify your guardian."

We both turned to him, my stomach in my shoes, and Tommy's face went completely pale.

"You know the rules," Mr. Abrahams said. "Pastor Kendrick is explicit about not allowing the students at St. Jude's to fraternize. You're not allowed to be in the same classes, much less…this."

"It was a kiss, Mr. Abrahams," I said, fighting down the blush I could feel climbing my cheeks. I tried to laugh like it was no big deal, but all of this felt like a very big deal. Too big a deal. "And it's not like Tommy did anything wrong. Teenagers kiss, Mr. Abrahams."

"Thank you for the newsflash, Beth," Mr. Abrahams said. "But if there's a reason he'd like to give me for why I shouldn't tell Pastor Kendrick, now would be the time."

This was our out! I looked at Tommy, nudged him with my elbow. He could tell Mr. Abrahams what went on at St. Joke's. How no one fed Tommy. And how Carissa barely talked. How Rosa had to pray on her knees every day, begging for forgiveness for her sins.

And the office.

Simon, Clarissa, Rosa and Tommy, they warned me…all the time. *Don't do anything that will get you taken to the office.*

The office was where bad things happened.

Tommy got taken there the first night I'd been at St. Joke's. And it was my fault he'd been punished, and he'd been left in bed for days afterward with his hands wrapped in bloody bandages.

"Tommy," I whispered.

"There's no reason," Tommy told Abrahams. "Do whatever you're going to do."

Tommy said it in just the right kind of voice that made Abrahams shake his head, oozing disappointment. I didn't get it. I didn't get any of it.

"Please, Mr. Abrahams," I said, feeling everything slip through my fingers. *I'd just gotten happy. Please don't take this away from us.* "I don't think you understand what it's like there—"

"Beth," Tommy said, his low voice cutting across mine. He shook his head, just a little. A hard no. But I remembered his hands, what The Pastor had done to him. On account of me. And I understood that none of us said anything about what happened there, because we were scared.

Scared of juvie.

Of The Pastor.

Of everything.

And it wasn't right. Or fair.

"Tommy, Beth." Mr. Abrahams stepped towards us. He dressed like a dad on TV. Khaki pants and button-down shirts, but he always wore really crazy socks, and when he stepped towards me I saw that they had emoticons on them. Little emoticon socks.

Surely we could trust a guy who wore emoticon socks, right?

"Is there something you need to tell me? About St. Jude's?"

He said it like he knew, and I opened my mouth to answer—to yell, actually: *Yes! Yes! There is! There's something evil and rotten and none of us talk about it because we're so scared.*

But Tommy beat me to it.

"No," he said in that serious, far-too-old-to-be-sixteen way he had. "There's nothing we need to tell you. But when you tell Pastor Kendrick, tell him it was me breaking the rules, not Beth."

"Tommy—"

The bell rang and he opened the door.

"We need to get to class," he said and pulled me out into the hallway, into the river of other kids heading from lunch to their next class. We got caught up in the current and I wished, I wished so badly that we could just keep going. That these kids with their normal lives and regular problems could just sweep us up, out the doors into the world away from everything.

"Tommy," I said. "Why didn't you tell him?"

"Because who is going to believe us? He's a pastor with a church and everything. He's been running this foster home for years. All we are is fuckups. Trouble kids."

That wasn't what we were. Rosa, Carissa, Simon...Tommy. *Especially Tommy.* We weren't fuckups. We were kids, and everyone who was supposed to take care of us—didn't.

"I don't believe that. I don't believe that at all. We should have told him. He knows something is wrong."

"Carissa tried to tell a teacher once."

I stopped, because his voice made the hair on my arms stand up.

"What happened?"

"She got sent to some hospital, came back on these meds that fucked her up, and she stopped talking."

"Why?"

"Why did she stop talking? Because talking got her in some serious shit—"

"No. Why did they take her away? Why didn't they believe her?"

"You're not like us, Beth. In your world, people believe you when you talk. The world doesn't give a shit about the rest of us."

I never told anyone what my mom did to me. It was a secret I kept because she'd made me think no one would believe me. That I was sick and untrustworthy and everyone knew it. The idea that someone would *listen* to me was radical.

Like I had superpowers I didn't know about.

"I should have told him, then," I whispered, turning back to the art room, where Mr. Abrahams stood watching us from the door.

"No way." Tommy pulled me away. "And then you'll get sent to a hospital. And you'll get put on some kind of fucked-up medicine."

I stumbled along after him, scared because my mom was the kind of doctor that put kids on fucked-up meds and I never told Tommy, but I'd been on my share. And I never wanted to do that again.

"I'm scared, Tommy."

I was scared and I was freaking out and I was so fucking mad at my mom I could barely breathe. This was her fault. All her fault. All her shitty lessons.

"It's going to be okay," he said. And he tried to be convincing, he did, and I would love him forever for it. "We've got each other. We're gonna be okay."

But he was lying.

2

That Night
St. Jude's School for Court-Placed Delinquents
Beth

WE WERE IN the kitchen after dinner. The girls cleared and washed dishes while the boys sat with The Pastor as he picked his teeth and asked them questions about school. It didn't seem like Mr. Abrahams had said anything. Everything tonight had been normal.

Except they let Tommy have the same food as us. As much as he wanted.

Which should have made me happy. Should have made me ecstatic, but it only made me feel like someone was stepping on my stomach.

Rosa was washing, I was drying, and Carissa was clearing the table, bringing in stacks of dinner plates and setting them down on the counter without a sound.

"What the hell is going on with you two?" she

whispered. We were good at whispering at St. Joke's, we were practically telepathic, that was how quiet we were.

"Nothing."

"Bullshit. They fed him and you didn't eat barely anything."

"I'm fine," I said, because that was what I was used to saying. It was what people liked to hear from me. That I was fine. When inside I was a black hole. Negative space. I was worry and I was fear.

And I was so much anger. I wanted to shatter every fucking dish in my hand, just smash it against the counter until the floor was filled with glass shards and The Pastor and his wife would be cut to ribbons.

But I didn't do that. Instead, I wiped dry every bowl and put them in the cupboard where they belonged.

Carissa came in with the bowl of cooked carrots and a stack of plates scraped clean.

"Here," she said, handing me a miniscule piece of folded-up paper. Tommy must have tucked it under his plate. The note-passing system at St. Joke's was next-level.

I opened the paper and read his tiny block letters.

Tell R and C. Everyone needs to be careful.

I put the note in the garbage and Rosa leaned over

and dumped the water that had been in the bottom of the bowl of carrots over the note, pretty much destroying it.

"Something happened today," I whispered.

"No shit," Rosa said.

"At school Abrahams caught Tommy and me kissing."

Carissa put her hands over her face and Rosa turned away to the sink, her head bowed. In the heavy echo-y silence I realized again how serious this was. And I felt like my head was going to explode from the tears and the fear I was holding back.

"You should never have started shit with Tommy," Rosa said. "For real. This is gonna hurt us all."

I swallowed back my apology, unwilling to be sorry for how I felt. Tommy and I were the only good thing I'd had in my life, and I wasn't sorry. But in the end I was just the kind of person who had to apologize. It was second nature. "I'm sorry. I just…I really like him."

Rosa said, real quiet, "I get it. I know what it's like to not be able to keep your hands off someone." She turned sideways as if making her point with the bump of her stomach.

"Girls?" The Wife came into the doorway, her face backlit by the light from the hallway behind her. I thought, as I had for probably the hundredth time, that her disguise was so complete. She looked nothing like a monster.

"Is there a problem?"

"No problem," Rosa said, smiling over her shoulder, her hands back in the soapy water.

"Good. Once you're done, you have homework in the church."

"The church?" The words fell from my mouth without thought, and Rosa stiffened next to me. Usually after dinner we all did homework together at the table, but questioning The Wife was a bad call.

"Rosa," The Wife said, "I think Beth can finish washing and drying the dishes on her own, don't you? Go get your schoolwork. Carissa, finish clearing the table and meet us in the church."

Rosa left, shooting me a *for god's sake keep your mouth shut* look over her shoulder.

I stared down at the heap of dishes I was going to have to do on my own, and I had a report due in World Studies. Shit.

Carissa came back in with the platter and all the cutlery.

"Maybe nothing will happen," I whispered, hope making my voice crack.

Carissa laughed, low in her throat. "Something will happen," she said, and it was so shocking to hear her talk my mouth fell open. "And when it does"—she leaned forward right into my space, her eyes glittering and hard—"fight."

3

That night
St. Jude's School for Court-Placed Juveniles
Tommy

THE DREAM WAS Beth. The dream was always Beth.

We were under the crab apple tree at school. Our tree.

I mean, dozens of kids sat there, but it was our tree. And she had her sketchbook and I had her.

That was all I needed. Ever.

In the dream, her hair was loose, which was how I knew it was a dream. I'd never seen her hair loose, she always had it pulled back in really tight buns or ponytails.

"What are you looking at?" she asked and then she smiled, revealing the way her two front teeth leaned just slightly against each other. Not crooked, but not straight either.

"You," I said.

"Well, stop. You're supposed to be looking over

there." She pointed with her bitten pencil to the lunch tables on the far side of the quad.

"I want to look at you."

Beth had freckles scattered like stars across her creamy skin, caught even on her lips and eyelids. She hated them, I knew. Her red hair and her freckles. But I wanted to put my lips against every one of them and whisper *thank you, thank you for being here.*

"You said I could draw you, remember? And I can't draw you like this."

"I think I lied." I felt the smile spreading across my own mouth and I still wasn't used to it. Smiling felt weird. I was sixteen and I don't think I'd ever in my life smiled as much as I did with Beth.

I leaned in to kiss her, but she put her free hand against my chest, burning through my shirt.

"Did you hear that?" she asked, looking over my shoulder. Her smile was gone and I wanted to tease that smile back. The sun was suddenly gone too and we weren't under the crab apple tree, we were in the art room and I shook my head, fighting with everything in me to stay in the dream.

"Tommy. Wake up. You heard that."

I did. I heard that. But I didn't want to. I didn't want to wake up. I wanted to stay in this art room forever.

"Tommy," she whispered. "Please."

I opened my eyes, the dream shattered, my skin trying to hold on to the sensation of her hair against my palm. The taste of orange Skittles on my tongue. My brain to the sound of her voice. But it was gone.

I lifted my head from the thin pillow that smelled like someone else's sweat, and listened.

The house was the same eerie quiet it always was.

But that sound... Something woke me up. Pulled me away from the magnet of Beth.

I glanced over my shoulder to see the lamp on over the desk. Simon was sitting there—of course—all his books open in front of him but he was turned, looking at the door.

"Did you hear something?" I asked.

Simon's glasses caught the lamplight and I couldn't see his eyes, so I couldn't see what he was thinking. Not that I ever knew what that guy was thinking. He could cut open his head and show me his brain and I'd still be fucking clueless about that guy.

"You," he muttered. "Having a wet dream."

"Fuck off," I muttered. But I put my hand under the covers, checked to make sure. Hard dick. No come. *Phew.* I hadn't meant to fall asleep, but my stomach had been full for the first time in months. It wasn't sleep as much as a food coma.

"You heard something in the hallway."

"No," he said and turned back to his books.

"Did someone knock? One of the girls?"

"It…wasn't a knock."

"Was it Beth?"

"Jesus," he muttered. "What is it with Beth?"

Everything was the answer. It was everything with Beth.

"You're going to get all of us in trouble," he said.

I felt like shit that he was right.

They let me have dinner, as much as I wanted. Which was ominous as fuck. And then—after dinner— we'd been split up all night.

Also ominous as fuck.

But the worst thing was The Pastor… The Pastor had that look in his eye.

The look that made me cold in my skin. The look that made me want to find safe places for everyone to hide. That look made me want to be a million feet tall, and wide and strong enough to stop him from hurting anyone.

But he would come after me. He liked coming after me the most.

I made sure of that.

"She might be having another nightmare." I put enough scorn in my voice to make sure Simon understood he was being an asshole.

She had nightmares. Every night. She and Rosa shared the room next to ours and we could hear her screaming sometimes, crying others. Rosa always knocked on the walls—three short fast knocks—letting us know she was okay, that nothing bad was happening. Well, nothing worse. Because being here was pretty bad.

Beth said she didn't remember what was so awful in her dreams, but mostly I think she didn't want to talk about it.

None of us wanted to talk about the shit that came to us at night.

I lay there listening, trying not to feel all the walls in this place. All the walls between me and Beth.

There was a knock on the wall from Carissa, who had the room on the other side of us. Two fast knocks.

I knocked back three times.

Everything okay?

Fine.

But not really. And we all kind of knew it.

Any minute The Pastor was going to come for me.

Simon closed one big heavy textbook and opened another.

"It's after one, dude," I said, picking a fight because I was so on edge. "What are you doing studying?"

Simon didn't say anything. He didn't say shit. Ever. He studied and he kept his head down and he didn't get in trouble or get involved in any of the scary business that went on in this place.

His dad had been an immigrant from Pakistan, married his mom, had Simon, was living the American Dream, but then a few months ago he lost everything in some shady business deal. His dad killed his mom and then shot himself.

Murder-suicide for real.

It was fucked up and I was ready to cut the guy some slack on it, but Simon looked away when some pretty heinous shit went down in this place. And that I cut no slack with. No one here was going to take care of us—we had to do it ourselves.

But Simon walked around like he didn't see any of it. And worse—didn't care.

Also—he was some kind of genius, so on principle I hated him.

"You know we share a room," I said. "How am I supposed to sleep with your fucking lamp on all the time?"

"You were sleeping just fine—"

The sound came again and I could identify it now because I wasn't sleeping.

Not a scream.

It was the sound of a scream cut off before it could get started. It was a sound a thousand times worse than a scream, and all the hair on my body stood up. A door shut and there were footsteps walking down the hallway away from our room. Away from the girls' room next to ours.

There was heavy thump. The footsteps stopped for a second and then started back up.

"That was from Beth and Rosa's room, wasn't it?" Simon whispered.

I said nothing, staring out the window at the bright white light of the streetlamp. When I first moved here I pretended it was the moon. Like the moon out the window of the apartment I'd shared with my mom. Like the moon outside the bedroom in my first foster home.

"Shit," Simon whispered.

He didn't come for me. He came for Beth.

And I just sat there. We both did. We sat there doing nothing.

When I curled my hands into fists and I could still feel the scars, the rough papery skin over my palms like burns that never went away from my last trip to the office after the graham cracker incident.

The scars matched the ones on my back. Across my ass.

Simon probably had the same ones.

The office was a fucked-up place where fucked-up shit went down.

As bad as my punishments were, I had this sinking fear that when the girls got taken to the office they got something different. Something worse. Carissa said when he took her all he wanted to do was pray with her, but I was pretty sure that was only part of the story. She left the worst of it out.

There was another thump and then a sob.

Silence.

All at once, I couldn't fucking take it. Not for another night. Another second. He had us so scared we couldn't stand up for each other. He had us so terrified we couldn't tell anyone what he did to us. How we were treated.

For years I'd kept my mouth shut, told myself half the time that I deserved what The Pastor did to me. Or I didn't deserve any better.

But I couldn't sit here, staring at these walls, and pretend nothing was happening. Like I did when Simon got taken. When Carissa got taken.

The way they pretended nothing was happening when I got taken.

Not again.

Because Beth fucking deserved better.

I charged for the door even though I knew it was locked. Locked on the outside. Like it was every night. We were trapped inside.

I grabbed the doorknob with both hands and rattled the door as hard as I could, but nothing budged. In this old fucking shithole of a house, the doors had all been reinforced. I braced both feet against the wall and pulled as hard as I could. And then I put my shoulder against the door and pushed as hard as I could. Nothing. Not any movement.

"What are you doing?" Simon asked.

"What does it look like?"

"Like you're being an idiot."

"I need to help her," I said, straining against the door, counting all the ways I'd made this happen. I knew the art room was a bad idea, but Beth just had to smile at me and I didn't care about anything but her.

This was my fault.

"You gonna fucking help me or not?" I said to Simon, but I knew he wasn't going to help. He was going to sit at that fucking desk pretending no one was getting hurt in the other room.

I was so sure of that, that when Simon showed up at my shoulder, I nearly jumped out of my skin.

"The hinges," he said. "They're on the inside of the door. If we can get those off—"

"With what?" I asked, even though it was a great fucking idea. "We don't have any tools in here, Simon."

He ran the three steps back to his desk and pulled open his book bag.

"If you have a screwdriver in there I'll take back every single shit thing I've ever—"

He pulled out a metal protractor. The thing nerds used in high-level math class. Disappointment bottomed me out.

"Are you kidding me?"

"It's what we've got." He pushed me out of the way so he could get down on his knees and start trying to pry open or unscrew or who the fuck knows what to get the hinges off the door.

I ran to the window, which was locked and sealed. Every kid who came to St. Joke's figured that out the first night, when they tried to run away from this place. Jacob, a kid who was here when I got here, he broke a window open one night and the cops came and took him away.

Last I heard he was down in San Bernardino serving four years.

The door slammed at the end of the hallway, and Simon and I both looked at each other.

"It's Beth, isn't it?" Simon asked. "What's he doing—"

"You know what he's fucking doing," I sneered, guilt chewing a hole right through me. "Hurry the fuck up."

"It's not..." Simon shook his head. "The hinges have been sealed with something. I can't do it."

I grabbed Simon's chair, lifting it over my head.

"What the hell are you doing?" he asked, getting up off his knees, coming at me like I was the problem.

"I'm going to throw it through the window—"

"And then what? We're on the third floor!"

"I'll climb down!"

"You'll fall and break your neck."

"So we do nothing!" I whisper-shouted. "I can't do nothing anymore! He's hurting her."

"You don't know that. Not for sure."

"What happened when he took you into the office after that shit with the candle?"

His face got red and he looked away because none of us talked about what happened in that office. And it wasn't just because he said if we told we'd lose our court placement and go to jail. I mean, we were all scared of that.

But if we all pretended like it didn't happen, then we could believe that it didn't happen. We could just put it away. Hide it someplace where we didn't look at it, think about it, and never…*ever*…talked about it.

It was the only way we could survive this place.

Not talking about it meant not going crazy with it.

The sound of a key in the lock of the door made both of us go still. I could feel my blood turn to ice, like it was cracking in my veins. We'd been whispering but we'd still been too loud.

"Fuck," Simon breathed, his dark eyes wide. "It's him."

Or worse. *Her.*

"I hope so," I whispered and tiptoed to the far side

of the door, the chair still in my hands. I'd fucking kill him if I had to. And her. I'd kill them both.

I wasn't some genius like Simon, I didn't have someone who loved me like Rosa. My future was as shitty as my past. And jail for killing *him* would be worth it.

The door eased open and Simon stood at the end of my bed, his wide eyes darting from me to the door and back again. I lifted the chair over my head, wondering how hard I'd have to hit him to kill him. I was pretty big and I would use all of my strength and I'd hit him as many times as it took. I locked my knees. Swallowed down the vomit in my throat.

I'd done some shit, but nothing like this.

I saw the toe of a shoe on the floor and I swung the chair in a wide arc around my shoulder, hoping to hit the fucker in the face.

"Stop!" Simon put his hand up and caught the swing of the chair that I tried to check but couldn't stop. Simon grunted as the chair hit his shoulder, knocking him back towards the bed.

I turned, ready to charge, but…it was Rosa at the door.

Rosa. Out of her room.

It was so strange I could only blink at her.

She had her black hood up over her long hair. The baggy sweatshirt she wore pulled taut over her pregnant belly.

"I'm out," she whispered. "I'd rather be in jail than here."

"How'd you get our door open?" I asked, my voice as low as I could make it. I knew Rosa had a whole history with B and E, but getting out of these rooms was no joke. Not when he locked the door from the outside.

She held up a key ring with five keys on it. "Fucker's not as careful as he could be when he's excited about raping teenage girls."

My stomach curdled.

"Did he just drop them in your room?" Simon asked. "The keys—"

"You got bigger problems than how I got the keys," Rosa said. "He just took Beth. You've got time before shit gets real."

This place needed to be burned down to the ground, and I'd be the guy to do it. Right after I found him and killed him. I'd light a match and watch it all burn.

And the memory would keep me warm in jail for the rest of my life.

I stepped past Rosa into the hall. Five doors. Ours was open. So was Rosa and Beth's. Carissa's on the other side was opened too. There was another locked and empty bedroom, and then his office at the end of the hall.

I stepped towards the door, the keys in my hand. They had those colored plastic things around the edges. A different color for each key. All I could think was:

He has us fucking color-coded?

"Wait," Simon whispered. "If you try a bunch of keys in the lock he'll hear you. You need to know which one is the right one."

Solid. That was solid thinking. But my fingers were shaking so hard I couldn't even separate one key from the ring.

"Hey," Simon stood beside me, his hand out for the keys. "Let me help you." I dropped the keys in his hand, never expecting when I woke up three minutes ago that I'd be grateful to him.

There was a creak on the stairs and we all went totally still.

The Wife.

When I first got placed at St. Joke's I had a baseball bat. My first foster family gave it to me, but the second I got to St. Joke's, The Pastor took it away.

A kid like me with a bat, he'd said, shaking his head.

And I'd thought, yeah, no shit. Who in their right mind trusts someone like me with a bat?

I wanted that bat back with everything in me. I

could do some damage with that bat.

Every muscle tensed, I figured I would just charge when she got to the top step. Push her down the steps and hope for the best.

The top step creaked like it always did and I bounced on my tiptoes, ready to charge. I was light-headed and shaking but I was ready to do this.

But it wasn't The Wife coming up the stairs.

It was Carissa in her pale pink pajamas. The moonlight coming through our bedroom door turned the long butcher knife in her hand to silver.

Relief made me nauseated. Adrenaline made me numb.

I collapsed against the door, sucking in air.

Carissa was the youngest of us. The smallest. That knife was half the length of her leg.

"Open the door," she whispered, all murderous business. Well, as much as a fourteen-year-old half-Chinese girl in a pair of pink pajamas could mean murder business.

Which was a lot, actually.

Simon, who'd been checking the keys, lifted one in the air. "Got it!"

"I'm out," Rosa said, her hand over her stomach, and none of us blamed her.

She and Carissa hugged briefly and Rosa was gone like she'd never been there at all.

"Give me the knife," I said to Carissa. "I'm bigger." I was bigger than Carissa, sure, but I was way smaller than The Pastor. I was tall, but he had a hundred pounds on me, easy.

I had the element of surprise and not much else going for me.

"I'll get Beth," she said and I nodded. Yes. Someone would need to see to Beth.

"You can't kill him," Simon said.

"I can't?" Because I could. And killing him was the plan. The scars on my hand burned like they agreed.

"You'll go to jail."

"Dude," I sneered, "I'm going to jail anyway. Now or years from now, it don't matter." Jail was the natural course of things for a kid like me.

"Yeah, but murder?"

"You don't want to do this, fine. Go back to your books. No judgement, Simon. For real. You helped a lot. But me and Carissa can do this on our own."

Carissa had been at St. Joke's before I got here, and she ran this shit. There wasn't a thing that happened in these walls that she wasn't fully on top of.

And she stood next to me at this door like she had no plans on bailing.

There was a thump on the other side of the door and Simon swore under his breath. But his fingers... man, they were rock solid. I was shaking like a leaf, but

Simon was steady. He put the key in the lock and slowly, silently, turned it. The door popped open and then eased forward.

And I knew in the pit of my stomach that whatever I saw in this room, whatever horror Beth was experiencing, it was on me. I'd known we were going to get caught. But I didn't care. I only cared about her. And how it felt when we were together.

I'd lost my head over her.

Don't look, I told myself. *Don't see.*

But it was impossible not to. The reality of it was so big. So horrible.

I saw the way her bare toes tried to get a grip against the floor. Her nightgown was pushed up to her thighs. Her knees thumped against the solid wood of the desk. Her hair was loose, the curls kinky and wild across the desk where she was pushed on to her stomach. The Pastor had one hand over mouth but I could hear her muffled screams. Her panicked breaths.

Her amber eyes, when they saw me, they opened wide and I read a thousand things there.

Fear and pain and a relief so wild she started to sob.

I roared when I was supposed to stay silent. I fucking screamed and I gave him warning, that we were here, that I was coming for him. He turned, pushing himself away from her, and I saw his open belt but couldn't tell if his pants were open. If he'd raped her or only planned on raping her.

And it didn't fucking matter.

I lifted the knife and charged him. He brought his arm up just as I slashed at him with the knife and felt the thick give of skin and muscle as the blade went through his hand. I tried again. To get his belly this time, that sickening wobble of it under the clothes he wore, and I hit something, felt him grunt and heard him swear, and then he punched me.

He hit me so hard I fell sideways, nearly losing my grip on the knife. I shoved at him, with all my strength, the knife cutting across his hand.

"Tommy," he said. "Put down the knife."

"No!"

"Put down the knife, Tommy, or this will not go well for you."

"Fuck you!"

He pushed me into the chair like I was nothing. Like I was a bug. Like all my fear and all my worry were made of air. The hate I felt for him was weightless.

"Tommy!" Simon yelled and I glanced up just as a thundering punch caught me across the face, making my ears ring and my eyes cross. There was another and another. I felt my nose pop, blood rushing into my mouth. I fell to my knees. And then to my side.

Carissa got Beth off the desk and into the hall, I saw

that. I saw Beth screaming and reaching for me, but Carissa was stronger than she looked and she pulled Beth away.

She was safe.

The Pastor kicked me and there was a crack and a bright white-hot pain in my side. A rib, probably.

I couldn't do this. Black was seeping into the sides of my vision. I pushed the knife across the floor where it skidded to a stop in front of Simon, who was watching me, horrified.

I tried to will Simon into grabbing that knife and charging at The Pastor while he was occupied with killing me. But as my chin came up The Pastor kicked me in the face, snapping my head back, and the lights went out.

4

Still that night
Tommy

B ETH SANG. LIKE really sang. Like for real. She didn't say much, not for that entire first week, but that first Sunday in church… Jesus.

The Pastor made us come every Sunday, trotting us out like prize fucking pigs in front of his congregation so they could all feel so good about donating money to us poor homeless kids with nowhere to go and no one to love us.

Whatever. Jackoffs.

Beth sat beside me, her hair in two of the tightest buns I'd ever seen at the back of her head. So tight it had to hurt. She wore a khaki skirt and a navy blue sweater and pretty boots that cost more, I'd guess, than every piece of clothing I'd ever owned.

Beth didn't make any sense at St. Joke's.

Like all of us she'd been court-ordered here, which meant she'd been in some kind of trouble. Word was, something had happened with her mom, and she'd split or Beth had run. None of us knew.

Beth had shown up in nice clothes and good shoes—none of them hand-me-downs. She'd even had pearl earrings. So you knew something was up with her life before St. Joke's. But she didn't say shit. Not about what got her there. Or her mother. Or the pearl fucking earrings.

Every day she got quieter and quieter.

Until church.

That Sunday, my hands were still red and swollen from the beatings. I couldn't hold anything, or think of much past the beat of my heart in my fingertips, but I'd felt her, all along my left side like a heater turned up too hot.

None of us sang. He could make us hold the hymnal and punish us for not standing, but if we all just sort of moved our lips, he didn't know we weren't singing.

It was pretty bullshit, but we had to get our rebellions in where we could.

But Beth had pulled out that hymnal and turned the pages to the right song so fast she actually tore one of thin parchment pages. Simon glanced up at the sound and winced. Damaging the church's stuff was bad news—Simon had firsthand knowledge of that after the candle thing a few weeks ago.

But Beth didn't stop. She didn't even seem to notice. She got to the right song, lifted her chin, and when the organ started she opened her mouth and…I don't know. I don't have the words to describe what that sound was like.

Angels is stupid and wasn't really true because there was something gritty in her voice, something that sounded how all of us felt deep inside. Lost and hurt and so fucking angry we couldn't breathe sometimes. That was it: she sounded angry.

Everyone in the pew—Carissa, Simon, and Rosa—everyone turned and looked at her, their mouths open. We were all feeling the same thing when she sang. Like somehow—out of nowhere—we had a voice.

It was crazy. I know. But we didn't have shit in that place and now…now we had that voice.

I couldn't explain what happened inside of me. It was like… everything shifted, you know. Like all my energy and thoughts and worry, they went from me…to her. Just like that.

By the end of the song I was pretty much in love with her. Maybe not love… I mean, what did I know about love? But I knew that if push came to shove, it was her before me. Every time. Not sure why. Or how.

It just was.

"Tommy! Tommy! Open your eyes! Please open your eyes!"

Someone was hissing in my ear and I understood that I wasn't in church with Beth. That I was somewhere else and I was… God, I was in so much pain. Everything hurt. My ribs were so bad I could barely breathe. The best I could do were little tiny sips of air.

I wanted to stay in that dream. That memory. No pain there. Just Beth singing and warming up one side of my body from a half a foot away.

"Tommy! Beth needs you!"

I opened my eyes as best I could, which meant one eye kind of opened. The other not so much.

"Oh, thank God." It was Simon, next to me. "Your breathing is so shallow, man, I thought you died."

I lifted my hand to try and touch my eye, but my hands were handcuffed to the chair I was sitting on. Simon was next to me in the same situation. Across a small table sat Carissa. She was handcuffed too.

And her pajamas were covered in blood.

Oh. Shit.

I gagged and it hurt so bad I almost passed out.

"Where's Beth?" I asked, clinging to the thing that mattered most.

"We don't know," Simon said.

"Don't… know?" I gasped.

"The ambulance came and they took her away."

Ambulance? Was that bad? Or good? I decided good because it meant she wasn't here and she wasn't dead.

"Where… are we?" I asked. The room was totally bare. Four chairs. One table. A two-way mirror on one wall. Well, shit. Stupid question. I'd been in enough police interrogation rooms to recognize where we were. The smell alone—bleach not doing its job against bitter coffee and vomit. "Who called… the police?"

"She did," Carissa said, looking out the small window of the door. "His wife."

"What happened?" I asked, my eyes on Carissa's previously pink pajamas. "Is he dead?"

"We shouldn't talk about it," Simon said, looking at that big wall full of one-way glass. "They're probably listening."

"He's dead," Carissa confirmed, expressionless and still.

"Did you kill him?" I asked. I mean…it seemed obvious…all that blood. But I couldn't remember a fucking thing. I pushed the knife across the floor and he knocked me out.

Carissa opened her mouth.

"Don't!" Simon barked. "Don't answer that. For the love of God, don't…say another word."

Well, that seemed like legit legal advice.

Carissa must have agreed. She shut her mouth and turned again to look out the small window in the door. The bright rectangle of yellow light.

We were going to jail—the fact was as real as that door. As real as the handcuffs. As real as my broken face.

"Police brought us here," Simon said and I could tell he was still clinging to some kind of hope. Like his big brain would get him out of this. "We were all in separate rooms, I thought you'd been taken to the hospital. But about ten minutes ago, they put us in here with you."

"That's...weird, isn't it?" I asked, because my head was so fuzzy and as far as I'd ever experienced, divide and conquer was pretty much police procedure. Letting us sit in here together and get our story straight was not how this shit went.

"Listen," Simon said. "I don't know why they have us all together here. But it's fucking serious. So no one talks. Not to anyone who comes in that door."

I felt myself smile. Or try to anyway. Fresh blood flooded my mouth from a split on my lip. "You gonna...be...our lawyer?" I panted.

Simon's dark face flushed red. "We're in serious fucking trouble, Tommy."

Well, I was pretty sure that I was going to die, and that felt like all the trouble I could handle. But Simon... Simon had had big plans. He took his life and his future seriously. He was going to age out in a few months, take the government money and go to college.

Make a difference. It didn't take a genius to know he wasn't made like me. He was made for more than St Joke's. And dude deserved that. So did Carissa over there covered in blood. I'd remember her coming up those steps with the knife in her hand for the rest of my life. Standing beside me at the door.

Ride or die, that was Carissa.

"I'll tell them…it was me," I said. "Only…me."

"You were knocked out," Simon whispered. "You don't even know what happened."

"And it wasn't just you," Carissa said. "We did it together. All of us."

That shouldn't make me feel good. Shouldn't make me feel a little bit like I wasn't alone, dying handcuffed to a chair. But it did.

The door opened, finally, and we blinked at the brighter light it let in. God, my head felt like a helium balloon.

One man stood there, tall and thin and blond. He looked like a serious lawyer in a serious suit. He said something to someone behind him and then he walked in and shut the door behind him.

The silence in the room pounded. Cold sweat ran down my whole body.

"Are you a cop?" Simon asked, sitting up straight. I liked that he was speaking for us. I was shit at talking my way out of trouble. Simon had that kind of thing locked down.

The man sat down in the chair next to Carissa, unbuttoning his jacket as he sat. "I am not a cop," he said in a low voice. He glanced at all of us but did a kind of funny double take when he saw me. He had eerie-as-fuck pale gray eyes, and they narrowed like someone was going to be in trouble.

"Have you had medical care?" he asked.

"What does it look like?" Simon snapped. "This is police brutality and we demand a lawyer."

The stranger smirked at him.

"I'm fine," I wheezed, determined to give this man nothing.

"Clearly," the stranger said. He stood up and went back and opened the door. A cop followed him back in.

"I think the cuffs can be done away with," the stranger said.

"You're joking, right?" the cop asked, scowling at us like we'd shit on the floor.

"Do I look like I'm joking?"

"You know what these kids did?"

"I do. And I don't think them killing the man who abused them means they are about to go on a killing spree," he said.

We all looked at each other at the word *abuse*. What the fuck did this guy know?

"It's your fucking funeral," the cop said, and one by

one he unlocked our handcuffs. Simon immediately stood up, his back to the corner, rubbing his wrists.

I stayed slumped in the chair, because nothing really worked anymore. Not my lungs or my legs.

Carissa too stayed seated, her hands spread wide over the table.

"Where's Beth?" I asked when the cop left.

"The hospital," the stranger said. "Her mother is there."

Carissa, Simon and I all shared a brief look at that. Her mother was real. And finally showed up. Too fucking late. I wondered, in some faraway way, if that was good or bad, her mother finally showing up.

"Who are you?" Simon had his chin up like a proper street thug.

"My name is Bates," the stranger said.

"Is that supposed to mean something to us?" Simon asked.

"To you?" Bates looked at Simon in one long sweep of a glance. "No. But I work for a man named Lazarus."

"Oh shit. What does Lazarus want with us?" I asked. Because Lazarus was bad news. Lazarus was king of all the darkest parts of San Francisco. And if this guy worked for him—that was why we'd been put together in a room like this and how Bates got our handcuffs off.

Lazarus and his men had the kind of power that

could get shit like that done—even in a police station. Especially in a police station.

And if Lazarus was mad that we'd killed The Pastor tonight—we were dead. Finished.

Bates could be here to walk us out into the parking lot, put us into the trunk of some car, and we'd never be heard from again.

Distantly, behind all the pain, I felt fear. A lot of fear.

"Lazarus wants nothing to do with you," Bates said. "I'm here on my own business."

Weird, but that didn't make me feel any better.

"I know who you are," said Carissa. She was fucking chilling, sitting there in all that blood. "Who you really are."

The guy was unreadable, and he and Carissa just looked at each other for a long minute.

"Were you hurt?" he asked her in a quiet voice.

Carissa leaned forward and said through her teeth, "It's not my blood."

Fucking badass, our Carissa. Who would have guessed?

Watching Bates, I realized he wasn't too much older than us. I was sixteen, Carissa fifteen, Simon seventeen, Bates might have been twenty-five? Hard to say, but he was young.

If he was in Lazarus' kingdom, it didn't matter how

young or old he was, all that mattered was that he was brave enough, or crazy enough to kill for the kingdom.

"You a lawyer?" Simon asked.

"No," Bates answered calmly.

"We demand a lawyer." Simon's voice cracked and his glasses slipped down his nose and he pushed them back up with his wrist. He didn't look like a murderer. He looked like a spelling bee champion.

"A lawyer isn't going to help you." Bates crossed his legs at the knee and pulled a piece of lint from his pants.

"Then why are you here?" Simon asked.

"As you can imagine, you three are in a great deal of trouble. The thin ice you were on as court-placed minors is broken. The prosecutors would like to try you all as adults for first-degree murder."

"It was me," I said, gasping. It was really getting harder to breathe. My vision was gray at the edges. "All me. They didn't do shit. Look at him," I said, tilting my head towards Simon. "He's going to be a fucking accountant. And she..." My head rolled listlessly towards Carissa. I hoped this was enough because this was all I fucking had. "Tried to stop me."

"That's a very noble lie you're telling," Bates said.

"Fuck you. I'm not lying."

He didn't believe me.

I opened my mouth to keep arguing but Carissa

interrupted. "Just…shut up, Tommy."

"I'm afraid the man you killed, his wife has told everyone who will listen that that the three of you acted together. That you planned it, and you planned on killing her and robbing them and the church."

"That's not true!" Simon cried.

Bates shrugged. "That is something you are welcome to prove in court."

Again, Simon, Carissa and I looked at each other. We knew how this would go. A public defender who wouldn't bother to learn our names would represent us, and it would be considered a success if we weren't gassed when we turned twenty-one.

We'd grow old in jail. Get out as middle-aged adults with our GEDs and a black mark by our names.

"This can't be happening," Simon moaned and I felt bad for him. I did. He should have stayed at his desk.

"It doesn't matter," Carissa said. "The system is made up of people like us. Wrong thing for the right reasons and no money to defend ourselves."

If I survived my injuries, I was going to jail. And I couldn't say it wasn't worth it. I was too late to stop him from hurting Beth, hurting all of us really, but we'd paid him back. We'd brought some righteous vengeance down on him. I wondered what his congregation would think of that.

But these two…they deserved better.

I had to figure out how to get them out of this.

"However, I am here to present you another alternative," Bates said.

Simon perked right up and I wanted to tell him to calm the fuck down. To not be so eager to make a deal with the devil. Because this guy, in his slick suit, he was the devil.

It was as plain as could be.

"What's the alternative?" Simon asked.

"You can walk out that door. Free—"

"Why? How?" Simon asked, and Bates held up his hand to silence him.

"With the understanding that you owe me a debt. And when I come calling for payment on that debt, you'll do as I ask or you will find yourself right back in this room, only there will be no escape. And you will go to jail."

"But the statute of limitations—"

"I don't think you understand the nature of my power," Bates said, looking angry for the first time. Next to him, Carissa stiffened, her face creased in a quick taut panic. "I can free you from this room. From the very serious charges against you. I can wipe away the crime you've committed. The crime with witnesses and murder weapons found in your bloody hands. I can make that all go away. Do you honestly think for one moment I can't also settle upon your shoulders another crime, equally violent, equally disturbing, that you had nothing to do with?"

Simon wanted to argue, I could see it on his face. But this man got our handcuffs taken off. He got us put in this room together. He walked in and sat down like he owned this precinct.

"Dude," I groaned. "It's real. He's legit. Why do you think we've been put together like this? Not even questioned? That cop acted like he was his boss."

And if he worked for Lazarus, he had that kind of power and more.

Simon swallowed, his glasses catching the light from the hallway. He was having a hard time believing it, and maybe I would too if I wasn't about to pass out.

"What will we have to do for you?" Simon asked. "In the future."

"Whatever I ask."

"Will it be illegal?" he asked.

Bates smiled like a shark. "Probably."

Simon swallowed, his face gray.

"Listen," I said, feeling a horrible collar go around all our necks. "You don't want these two. I'll owe...you. Me. I'll work for you. Whatever you want."

"Tommy," Simon breathed. "No."

"Interesting," Bates said. "You know what I'll ask you to do, don't you? What it means to work for me?"

Killing, maybe. Hurting, definitely. Bile rose up in my throat but I nodded anyway. "Better…me…than…them."

Bates watched me for a long time and I tried to sit up straight as if to show how big I was.

"I'm growing…if…I got…enough to eat…"

Starving me was a favorite punishment of theirs. I had not been full in years.

"You'd be massive," Bates said, cocking his head. "But it's not your size that interests me. It's your loyalty."

"Tommy," Simon said. He touched my shoulder but I shook him off. "Don't do this."

"What about The Wife?" Carissa asked, pulling Bates' attention from me. "She witnessed everything."

"I can handle her," Bates said in a voice that sent chills down my spine.

"There was another girl," Simon said.

"Rosa." Bates nodded. And it wasn't even weird that he knew her name. I mean it was, but this guy was like God coming down and promising shit that didn't even make sense. Of course he'd know about Rosa.

"She might get in trouble—"

"I'm trying to find her," Bates said.

Rosa was good at disappearing, but I was still surprised he was trying. I could see Simon trying to swallow back all his questions and I totally understood.

I had plenty of my own.

"Will we have to go back into foster care?" Simon asked.

"That's not my concern," Bates said. "My deal only gets you out of these doors. After that, everything is up to you."

"They have to find us first, right?" Carissa asked. "The parole officers and social workers?"

"That's the view I would take," Bates said in his calm cool voice.

There were a thousand places in this city kids like us could hide. We'd be smarter this time. We wouldn't get caught.

Carissa got to her feet, her chair screeching across the floor behind her. "I agree to your terms."

"No!" I shouted and nearly passed out. "Don't, Carissa!"

"You didn't kill him, Tommy. This isn't your fault. I'm doing this."

Bates watched her out of the corner of his eye, like she was some unpredictable animal that might attack. It was the blood on her pajamas. Totally unnerving.

And just like that Carissa walked out of the room. I heard her footsteps down the hallway and no one stopped her. Not one cop. I imagined her walking out into the night. No cops. No foster homes. She would vanish just like Rosa.

I couldn't pretend I didn't want that freedom. I wanted it so bad I could taste it.

"So do I," I said. "I accept your terms. Leave Simon out of it." I got to my feet, ready to follow Carissa down that hallway, but the room spun around me and my knees buckled. Simon rushed to my side and helped me back into my seat.

"You need to get to the hospital," he said.

"I'll be fine," I said, swallowing down vomit. God, I was fucked up. Breathing was growing impossible.

"What about you, Simon Malik?" Bates looked at Simon. "Do you agree? Because it has to be all of you or none of you."

"Why are you doing this?" Simon asked, and I wanted to tell him to just shut up. To stop questioning everything.

Bates stood, buttoning his jacket, looking like a CEO and not a killer, though I knew he had plenty of blood on his hands.

He shook his head. Whatever the answer was to that question, he wasn't telling a bunch of kids. "Do you agree to the terms or should I have the police come in and start the booking process? At this point, you would be the only defendant. And that will not look good for you."

"Agree to the terms, Simon," I said. I'd lost the fight to keep my friends safe. We were all drowning together, tied to a killer named Bates. Jesus, the lights were suddenly getting brighter in here.

"I agree to the terms," Simon said.

And it was done. Our futures sealed.

Bates walked out, the door clicking shut behind him. It was weird...eerie how it felt like we'd dreamt him.

"Simon," I said. "I'm so sorry."

"Fuck off with that. We got bigger problems."

Bigger problems. And I caused them all.

Simon crept to the door and looked out the window.

"No one's coming," Simon said.

"We gotta get...out," I panted. Simon helped me to my feet and we lurched our way out of the police station. Waiting, every step, for someone to stop us.

But we pushed open the door and the sea salt air of San Francisco and the roar of traffic in the outside world felt like a goddamned hug.

"Let's get you to the hospital," Simon said.

"You...you don't have to come...with...me," I said.

"Yeah, because you can do it on your own?" he asked.

I couldn't. But Simon didn't make me say it. He just got me to the hospital.

I HAD TWO broken ribs. A broken nose and a concussion.

The hospital called the police, and about three hours after I got there, my parole officer showed up. The minute he left the room to make some calls, we got the fuck out of there.

It was Simon's idea to pocket as many samples of high-level Oxy as we could shove in our pockets, which he promptly sold on the street so we could rent a room in a shitty hotel in the heart of the Tenderloin.

We lived low to the ground. Under the radar of cops and the social workers who would be looking for us. The newspaper said that the pastor died of a heart attack. His wife was moved to a mental hospital. The congregation disbanded.

Simon couldn't claim the check for college he'd been counting on because he ran away. To get it he'd have had to go back into the system, and he had no time for that. He got his GED, applied for a shit ton of scholarships, and fuck if he didn't get a free ride to UCLA.

I got a job working construction and did my very best not to care. Like I'd used it all up in St. Joke's. Not giving a shit was a thing I perfected.

We didn't hear from Carissa. Not for years.

Rosa finally turned up, but it wasn't good.

And Beth…Beth just vanished.

Until it came time to pay the debt.

PART II

5

Seven years later
Tommy

I WALKED INTO Lucy's and held the door open for Pest, who came in behind me. Her prance was a little slower these days, so it took some time for her to get through the door, but she came, bell jangling, head up like the world was just waiting for her to walk in.

Pest was the walking embodiment of delusions of grandeur.

I'd said it a million times over the last six years she'd been with me, but she was a ridiculous fucking dog.

The bar was empty—the bar was always empty, which was why I liked this place better than any of the other pubs along my street. The gentrification of this far end of the Tenderloin had turned most of my usual spots into cappuccino bars and something called "gastropubs," which really only sounded gross.

But Lucy's refused to change.

I liked that about Lucy's.

It was dark inside the way bars were supposed to be, and the bar itself managed to be both smooth and sticky. There were small dips worn out on the edge from the millions of people who had braced their elbows against the wood after a long day. Sometimes I sat there and imagined the guys who built the bridge coming here after work, just a long line of workers like me.

Too tired to make their own dinners.

The booze was purely standard rail. The taps never changed, and the burger was the best and pretty much only thing on the menu.

All of this suited me down to the dust on my boots.

Lucy herself was behind the bar, and she threw a cardboard coaster in front of me. She and her family moved here from Puerto Rico when she was a kid, and her brother was a tattoo artist—her arms were solid sleeves of green vines and pink flowers. Puerto Rican flags on the backs of both her hands.

"Usual?" she said, and I nodded, pulling my phone out of my back pocket.

The sound was off on the TV above the bar, but the news ticker told the usual story in my city. Someone got stabbed. A police officer had been shot and was in the hospital in critical condition. The president was being an idiot, and some pop princess had passed out onstage during a concert.

"Is that a dog?" a blonde woman asked as she walked in from the back, where the tables were. Pest, sensing attention, wagged her bushy tail.

Pest got this question a lot because of her resemblance to a squirrel. Or maybe an overgrown rat. Pest looked like a lot of things—a dog wasn't really one of them. She had runny eyes and a snaggletooth and fur that didn't know which way it wanted to go.

"It is," I said as if surprised to find Pest beside my stool.

"Is that…allowed?"

"Service dog," I said.

"For real?" she asked.

Lucy shrugged and put a pint of Guinness down in front of me. "Social anxiety," she said. "I saw the letter from his doctor myself."

"Go figure," the woman said, patted Pest on the head, and walked down to the end of the bar to study Lucy's beer list.

I smiled and shook my head: Welcome to the Tenderloin, where no one questioned anything too hard.

Lucy winked at me before setting down a small bowl of water for Pest. I took it off the bar and put it on the ground by my stool. Lucy was a good egg. One of the best. I should have been kinder to her when she gave me the chance. One of about seven thousand regrets I lived with. Pest got up on her feet to go sip like a lady at the bowl. As a rule, Pest had better manners than me.

"Burger?" Lucy asked, and I nodded. She turned to punch it into the old computer system. "How's work?"

"Good," I said, rubbing my hands together, the sounds of the calluses audible in the room. My hands were a solid mess. Rough and fucked-up. I hated working with gloves, and all the fancy lotions didn't do much good after the fact. Such was the life of a mason, I guess.

My hands were my hands.

But the calluses covered up the old scars, which, maybe, was the point.

"What are you building these days?" she asked.

"Rich guy's driveway."

"Out of stone?" Lucy asked.

"Rich guy wants what rich guy wants."

"Rich guys," Lucy said with a shake of her head. "Plain burger for Pest?" she asked.

"Yeah, thanks."

She went to go serve the blonde at the other end of the bar.

"Would you mind turning that up for a second?" the blonde asked, pointing to the screen. Lucy reached over and unmuted the TV. "I want to see if they're going to give us an update on that cop that was shot."

"Pop sensation Jada," the television reporter said, and behind her flashed pictures of a young woman in constantly changing costumes. She was a mermaid and then a bull in a matador costume; then, unbelievably, a whole cotton candy costume. Once she was painted to look like a cloudy blue sky. "She's finished her North American tour in what has become typical dramatic fashion. The singer, known for her sexy costumes and out-of-this-world makeup, collapsed last night halfway through her show at the Hollywood Bowl. Sources say the Internet sensation turned global sex symbol is exhausted and will be taking some time off before heading to Europe."

"Drugs," the woman said, pointing at the TV. "Exhaustion is just code for drugs."

I looked down at my hands and ignored the lady and her flip fucking know-it-all attitude. I didn't come to Lucy's for conversation.

"In local news, family is rushing to the hospital to sit at the bedside of Officer Roger Martin. Martin was shot while sitting in his patrol car at the corner of Taylor and Seventh. Despite it being the middle of the day and a crowded intersection, no witnesses have come forward. Police are looking for any information the public might have on this crime."

On the bar my phone buzzed, and I turned it over to see a text from Simon.

Just landed in LA.

I felt the tension in the back of my head let go. The stress headache I'd been living with for three weeks vanished from behind my eye.

Welcome home, I texted. *Everything okay?*

I'm exhausted, starving, my luggage was lost and I think I have lice—so everything is great, he texted, and I smiled.

Simon was on a Pulitzer-Prize-winning team of journalists who'd covered the Ebola outbreak and the Syrian refugee crisis, and now he was working on the Russian influence in European elections.

Every time he left the country, there was a solid chance he wouldn't come back. He had enemies. Real enemies. Leaders-of-countries enemies. Enemies that didn't just jump a guy on his way back from a bar, but put plutonium in his tea.

He had assassin enemies.

But Simon was tough as fuck.

He just hadn't known it until that night. None of us had.

Gonna sleep for a day. Dinner tomorrow night?
Sounds good.
I'll drive up tomorrow. Later.

I put the phone back down on the bar, and Lucy smiled at me.

"Good news?" she asked. "You look lighter."

I felt fucking lighter.

"Friend is home safe is all."

Lucy pushed three full pints across the bar to the blonde and took her money.

"You told me you didn't have friends," Lucy said over her shoulder at me as she put the money in the till.

My face got hot. That was the line I'd given her that night a year ago when she'd asked me to her place and I'd botched the whole stupid thing. I had no fucking clue what to do when women looked at me, wanted that kind of thing from me. It made me nervous. It made me say stupid things like *I don't have friends.*

Which was true. But who says it?

"Relax, Tommy," she said. "I'm only teasing."

She turned the volume down on the TV. Back in the kitchen a bell rang, and Lucy went back, probably to grab my burger.

I'd been cutting and hauling granite and sandstone since six this morning; my neck was jacked. My arms ached. I rolled my shoulder, listening to the tendons snap, crackle and pop. I was one of the younger guys on the crew, and I tried to help out the old guys as much as possible. Paul was fucking forty and had lupus, and he was still hauling stone. It was nuts.

The front door opened again just as Lucy came in from the kitchen, carrying two plates. She paused in the doorway, looking as if she'd seen a ghost, and her expression was so weird I turned to see who'd walked in.

The door was open behind her so I couldn't get a look at her face, but the new arrival was dressed sharp. One of those tight skirts that came down to a woman's knee, that managed to look both sexy and classy all at once. Her black hair was cut razor-sharp to her chin, and the heels she wore were high.

Lucy put the plates down on the bar in front of me with a clatter.

"Everything okay?" I asked her in a low tone.

Lucy shook her head once and then turned to the woman, who had sat down two stools away from me.

"What can I get you?" Lucy asked with none of her usual friendliness. I put the plain burger down on the floor in front of Pest, but my dog was watching this new woman too.

She didn't look it, but Pest was a pretty good guard dog. I trusted her instincts about people, better than I did my own. I didn't like anyone. Pest didn't like lousy people.

"Gin martini," the woman said. Her head was tilted down, her hair hiding her face, but something in her voice pinged in my chest. Familiar. Really familiar.

Lucy made the drink and slid it across the bar. The woman put a twenty-dollar bill on the counter, and Lucy lifted her hand. "No charge."

"Thank you, Lucy," the woman said, again in that voice that pulled at something in my brain. "Perhaps there is something in the kitchen that needs your attention?"

I blinked in astonishment as Lucy nodded and disappeared through the kitchen door without so much as shooting me a glance.

Fuck. I was getting set up for something.

I turned to stare openly at the woman as she took a sip of her martini and then carefully placed it back down on her coaster. Lining the glass up with the small damp ring on the blue cardboard. Her skirt was black, and the silky shirt she wore was cream, and on top of that she wore a slim leather jacket. Her heels were leopard print.

And there was an alarming amount of danger around her. Like the air before a lightning storm. She was negatively charged, and all the hair on my body stood up in reaction. Every instinct told me to get up and leave.

"Hello, Tommy," she said.

I jerked back a little. "How do you know my name?"

"You don't recognize me?" she said, staring at the mirror behind the bottles. I glanced there too and saw her face. It was a beautiful face.

She was Chinese, and she wore bright red lipstick

and had diamonds in her ears, peeking through her jet-black hair.

"Should I?" I asked. Pest, at my feet, growled low in her throat, sensing that things were not right.

The woman turned to look at me straight on. "I was fifteen the last time we saw each other."

Fifteen.

Jesus.

"And I was covered in blood."

The penny dropped and nearly knocked me off my stool.

Ride or die.

"Carissa," I whispered.

She smiled, nodding slightly, the diamonds in her ears winking in the half-light of the bar. "It's good to see you, Tommy."

Other people maybe might have hugged at this point. But I wasn't a hugger, and she exuded a do-not-touch vibe that was as potent as an electric fence. The best I could manage was leaning forward, toward her, remembering the kid she'd been.

We'd been at St. Joke's the longest, her before me. But there was a part of Carissa that was unknowable. A deep, still lake with a bottom too far to ever reach. I thought, with a sinking stomach, that whatever had happened to her in that hospital had a lot to do with that.

"What…" I felt myself smiling, even though it wasn't exactly joy I experienced when I looked at her. I'd spent a lot of time putting those memories to bed, pretending, when I had to, that they never happened. But I couldn't deny the fact that it was good to see her, and looking like a highly polished diamond. She was stunning. And she looked so…clean.

I was smeared in our past; it hung off me like a parasite. The kind of thing I was sure people could see when they looked at me.

This guy, they'd think, is damaged goods.

But her? The past—our past—I couldn't see it on her. It was like it didn't even touch her.

"What are you doing here?" I asked.

"I'm here for you," she said. She got off her stool and came to sit next to me, bringing her martini with her. Pest growled half-heartedly, and I picked her up and put her in my lap to calm her down. She could get yappy when stressed out.

"Guard dog?" Carissa asked, eyeing Pest with one arched brow.

"She likes to think so."

"She's ugly."

"Yes, she is." I smiled despite myself. "You look good, Carissa."

"You," she said with a breathy laugh, "look completely different."

"Not that different." Embarrassed, I put my hand through my hair.

"Someone finally fed you. You look good, Tommy. Really good."

"That, we both know, is a lie." I had sandstone dust in my hair no matter how many times I washed it, and my neck was red from the sun. My hands... I put them around my beer.

"You were always so modest. I remember that about you, you know. That you were modest and that you tried to take care of everyone."

"Right."

"We were kids. And you did the best you could."

I cleared my throat and took a sip of my beer. Me taking care of everyone hadn't turned out well for anyone, really. "What happened to you after that night?" I asked. "We looked for you—"

"You and Simon." It wasn't a question; she knew we'd been looking for her. "I was surprised you two stayed in touch after that night."

"He took me to the hospital," I said. "I couldn't shake him after that."

It was a tired joke. A lame one, so far from the truth it was almost insulting.

"I had no interest in being found," Carissa said.

"Rosa—"

"I know," she said in hushed tones, because the

Rosa thing was a fucking tragedy. "She gets out soon."

"Beth?" I had looked for Beth for years. Simon had, too. And Simon had serious skills in that department. But Beth's mom had covered their tracks, and Simon thought she'd changed her name and the trail had gone cold.

Simon and I had lived for years waiting for the other shoe to drop from that night. But over time it started to feel like that night was a bad dream we'd shared. The only proof that it actually happened was the fact that we were friends. Because guys like us would not have crossed paths otherwise.

But Carissa was here, solid proof it had not been a dream.

"We are discussing you," she said.

I blinked. "Yeah? You need a stone mason or something?"

She pulled from her sleek black leather bag a big manila envelope, which she set on the bar and pushed across the wood toward me. It made a scraping sound, like nails across a chalkboard. "It's time for you to pay your debt."

The words were barely out of her mouth and I knew what she was talking about.

That night.

The debt.

I'd thought about this moment. I'd thought about it

so much I was sure I knew what I'd do, how I'd feel. I had a speech even. About how I wasn't that kid anymore and Bates could do whatever he wanted, but I wasn't going to hurt anyone for my freedom.

I wasn't worth it.

Tougher versions of the speech involved a fight and me going to jail so I didn't have to pay back any debt. I'd spend the rest of my life in jail, and maybe that would be okay. I worried about Pest in that scenario, but Simon could figure it out.

But in the reality of the moment, I didn't say any of my speeches.

And I didn't start that fight.

Because, *oh my God*…all I felt was relief. So much fucking relief my body went numb.

Just like when I'd been a kid and the cops caught me living on the streets. I'd fought. I'd fought as hard as I could, but inside…it was pure relief.

It's over. I can stop waiting for this shitty thing to happen because it's happening.

"You made a promise that night."

"I remember," I said. "What's in the envelope?" I jerked my chin at that envelope, unwilling to touch it until I had to.

"The favor Mr. Bates needs you to do for him."

"How bad is it?" I asked. My mouth was stone dry. I took a sip of my Guinness, but it did little good.

"Haven't you already learned that bad is relative?" Carissa said. "It's simply a matter of what you can survive."

I felt the old questions pull at me, the morbid curiosity of what had happened to her in that hospital.

How much have you had to survive?

But I swallowed those questions, because if she hadn't answered them then, the sleek, still woman in front of me definitely wouldn't answer now.

"That's what I'm worried about," I said. "Will I survive what's in that envelope?"

One thin shoulder lifted in a half shrug, and she took another sip of her martini.

Right. Message received. My survival was not the goal. Or even a consideration.

Still, I didn't touch the envelope. I didn't reach for it. It sat between us like a snake.

"You can't say no," she said. "You understand that, don't you?"

"I can say no; I just have to be ready to go to jail."

She sighed as if frustrated by me. "Did you watch the news?"

"I saw some of it."

"A cop was shot," she said. "Sitting in his squad car eating a sandwich. Someone walked up and shot him in broad daylight. No witnesses. No weapons on the scene."

"The cop's in critical condition," I said.

She glanced down at her watch. "As of fifteen minutes ago, he's dead."

"You're saying if I don't do what's in that envelope, that's what you'll pin on me?"

Cop killer.

I had the strange sensation of falling even as I sat there.

Carissa just watched me, her dark eyes giving away nothing.

"I think you're bluffing." I had no idea if she was bluffing, but fuck... that much power? How? This wasn't a fucking movie. It was life.

From her bag she pulled her cell phone and tapped away at the screen, her eyebrow arched like she was proving something to me. And then, just as she set down the phone, into the bar walked two policemen.

Two fucking policemen and they just stared at her. And she stared at me.

"Am I bluffing, Tommy?"

Mouth dry with adrenaline, I shook my head.

She turned and smiled at the men. "False alarm," she said, and they left without another word.

Jesus Christ.

I put a finger on the edge of the envelope, pulling it slowly toward me.

"You made the right choice, Tommy."

"I'm not… I can't hurt anyone. If what's in this envelope requires me to hurt someone, I'd rather go to jail."

"No one is getting hurt." She took a sip of her martini. "Not if you do everything we ask."

"We?" My stomach went sour. "You work for Bates? Is that how he made you pay your debt?"

She shook her head. "There is no debt involved."

The envelope had a rectangular bulge at the bottom, like a passport or some kind of ID. Another bulge next to it, a small thick square. Other than that, it was just a big pale brown envelope.

My size made people assume things about me. Guys would try to start fights with me just to see if they could take down the big guy. Even my job made people think they know something more about me than that I worked with stone. The way I talked, which admittedly wasn't great. The neighborhood I lived in. Girls, when they got to know me and I told them about the foster homes, they got this look in their eye that told me how they were filling in all the blanks. With violence. They were filling in the blanks with violence.

I'd avoided jail thanks to Bates, and after that I made every decision I could to stay out of trouble, because the world wanted guys like me to be in trouble.

It's hard not to be violent when the world pushes you toward it.

"I'm not interested in going to jail for a small crime just to avoid going to jail for a big crime."

I looked up and found her smiling at me, the twist of her lips sad and drenched in memory.

"I said that to Bates, but he thinks he has something that you'll believe is worth going to jail for if it comes to that."

I put my hand on Pest's head, feeling the bone beneath her skin. The velvet-soft fur of her ear, reliable comfort since I found her six years ago living behind a dumpster, surviving on scraps just like Simon and me.

"What's worth going to jail for?" I asked, braced for the worst.

"Beth."

Carissa stood up, drained her martini, and gathered her bag, all while I gaped at her.

"You know where Beth is?" I asked.

"This gets done tonight," she said, tapping the envelope. "And you don't get a second chance, not with Bates."

With that she turned and walked out the door, as sleek and as sharp as a blade.

And like a knife, she left me in pieces.

After all these years...

Beth.

6

Tommy

I LIVED ABOVE a pho restaurant off O'Farrell and Leavenworth, just behind one of the apartment buildings with the doorman. I was about three blocks west of the first apartment Simon and I had lived in after I got out of the hospital years ago.

We'd slept on the floor with the cockroaches, and we both got two jobs each, just so we could afford the one room. After Simon went to Los Angeles for school, I stayed there a little longer until I got the job working construction and made enough to move out. I'd been living in the same three rooms ever since. I could get a nicer place in a nicer neighborhood, but that seemed like a lot of work, and the Tenderloin was home. I wasn't sure I'd feel comfortable in another neighborhood. There weren't that many places in San Francisco that looked like me. *Felt* like me.

Pest stopped to investigate the edge of a building and some other dog's piss, but I whistled once at her and she abandoned her investigation. A cop drove by, nice and slow, just making the rounds through the neighborhood like they did every night. I felt that envelope, hot against my body where I had it tucked between my jacket and my shirt.

A shitty rumpled paper Pandora's box.

I hadn't looked inside it yet, but I had no doubt whatever was in it, it wasn't legal.

And it was going to unleash a shit ton of trouble on my life. It already had.

Part of me had wanted to open that envelope right there on the bar and find out where Beth was, but a strange burst of caution stopped me.

Caution and Lucy.

Lucy, after Carissa left, came running out of the kitchen, more shaken than I'd ever seen her—and I'd seen her break up some serious bar fights.

"How the fuck do you know her?" I asked Lucy, who, with shaking hands poured herself a shot of whiskey and knocked it back.

She held the bottle toward me, but I shook my head.

"How the fuck do you?" she snapped. She leaned forward over the edge of the bar, her voice dropped to a whisper even though the place was almost entirely empty. "There's been a pretty big shakedown around here and I don't know who she is or who she works for, but she is in it up to her neck. She scares the shit out of me."

You should have seen her seven years ago.

Lucy had dumped the burgers in a box and handed it to me, and I got the real clear message that me and Pest weren't welcome back if Carissa was going to be regularly joining me.

I'd left Lucy's wanting to say goodbye to her. Wanting to tell her that I appreciated all the kindness she'd given me all these years. That I was sorry that night I'd turned her down, that it had been a mistake.

I'd left Lucy's feeling like I'd never see her again.

The envelope, burning my skin through my shirt, was going to change everything.

Beth. After all these years, what was I supposed to do about Beth?

I'd put that night away. I'd put those feelings away like they belonged to a different person.

That kid who thought he loved a girl who was worlds better than him, that boy who thought he could save her, save everyone… That kid didn't survive the beating the Pastor gave him.

It was only me now, and I didn't care. I worked really fucking hard not to care.

I crossed the street to my apartment, walking past the front bumper of a shiny black German-made sedan parked in front. New, from the looks of it. Someone was being reckless parking it so close to the worst neighborhood in the city.

Pest made her way up the stairs to my apartment, one at a time, her tail wagging despite the effort of all those steps.

Inside I gave Pest her burger, breaking it into pieces in her bowl. "Sorry, girl, for making you wait."

I took my dinner—which I was no longer hungry for—into my living room and set it on my coffee table. I put the envelope next to it and sat down on my beat-up leather couch, the familiar creak of its old springs catching my weight.

Still, I didn't open the envelope. I turned it over. And then over again. Something in the bottom rattled.

Over the years I'd imagined Beth in about a million scenarios. Living a good life far away from this city and its memories. I imagined her with a boyfriend, some guy who treated her right, and I wanted to punch him in the face on principle. I imagined her putting St. Joke's and that night a million miles behind her.

I imagined her never, ever imagining me.

She got out of the hell where we'd met—the only place the two of us made any kind of sense—and she moved on.

Moved on. Novel fucking idea.

I tore open the envelope, turned it upside down, and let the contents fall onto the coffee table. Pest, done with her burger, came to sniff at mine.

"Go ahead," I told her, and like the delicate lady she was, she grabbed the burger in the corner of her mouth and flopped down to eat it at my feet.

On the table in front of me was a driver's license with my driver's license picture but a different name.

Sam Johnson.

"Jeez, Carissa," I muttered. "That's the best you can do?" *Sam Johnson* screamed *fake name*. I didn't even bother wondering how they'd gotten the DMV picture of me. Just another example of the power Bates carried in his pockets like spare change.

There was a limo service ID with my picture and Sam Johnson's name.

And there was a key. A BMW key fob. I had a strange chill in my stomach, and in the dark shadows of my apartment I went to my front window overlooking the street and the black BMW sitting in front. I hit the unlock button, and the lights blinked on.

The BMW was mine.

Fuck.

Back at the table I picked up the single sheet of printer paper. One side was blank, but when I flipped it over on the other side it said:

Pick up:
1139 Mission Ridge Rd Santa Barbara

Delivery:
1165 Tegner St
Sunshot, AZ
Delivery window 8-9 AM
Text DONE to this number when delivery complete

There was a cell phone number scrawled alongside.

I collapsed backward onto my couch, staring up at the lights from my front window cutting cross patterns through the shadows on my dark ceiling.

What was I supposed to be delivering? And what did Beth have to do with this?

Fuck. I had to be in Arizona by eight a.m. with a stop in Santa Barbara? I glanced at my watch; it was six p.m. now. I had to go. Like…now.

In my bedroom I threw a clean pair of jeans, some underwear, toothpaste and toothbrush, and a clean shirt in a bag. I also took a second to take off my dark Henley and put on a dress shirt and my only pair of dress pants. It was as close to looking like a professional driver as I could get. With my bag over my shoulder I turned to see Pest in the doorway, watching me with her tail wagging.

I'd be gone two days, barring something going wrong. I couldn't leave her alone for all that time.

Because something was probably going to go

wrong.

"Wanna go for a ride?" I asked, and she barked once in reply. "Let's go, girl."

I grabbed the stuff from the table and headed down to the car, which again lit up and honked when I hit the button. My work truck parked in back was going to feel like shit when this little joyride was over.

Work. Crap.

Inside the car Pest predictably called shotgun. Across the steering wheel was a black tie and a handwritten note pinned to it.

Was pretty sure you wouldn't have one of these—C.

Yeah, well, I didn't. Points to Carissa. I looped the tie around my neck but didn't bother tying it. I grabbed my phone and texted Paul from work.

Emergency. I won't be at work for a few days.

He texted back right away. *Emergency? With what?*

I nearly laughed. Right. What in my life had emergencies? Pest turned a circle in the seat and lay down with a flop on the fine leather seats. I imagined returning this car covered in dog fur, and it wasn't a bad thought.

Pest, I texted.

Crap. Okay. Let me know.

I smiled. Pest went to work with me every day, so

she was as much a part of the crew as some of the new guys. And I had enough goodwill built up that a few days off for my dog was not a big deal.

I mean, it was kind of a sad deal, that the only thing in my life was Pest. But whatever.

Crap. And Simon.

Dinner's off, I texted to him. *Will talk later.*

I pulled up an app on my phone and plugged in all the addresses to get the route.

I didn't expect an answer from Simon, but the text bubble appeared.

What happened? he asked.

I thought about lying. But I didn't lie to Simon. There was no point. And this… Fuck, if Bates was coming for me, he could be coming for Simon, too.

That old debt came due, I texted, feeling like that was the only safe thing to say. *Have to go.*

And do what? he wrote back. *How bad is it?*

Not sure yet, I texted. *But—I took a deep breath—it's about Beth.*

I put the phone down, put the car in gear and took off into the twilight, heading, it seemed, right back into my past.

7

Tommy

WE HAD AN elaborate note system in St. Joke's. Scraps of paper slipped under doors, tucked in the pages of Bibles, crumpled in hands that passed dirty dishes from the table to the sink. We were like a spy network constantly gauging the Pastor's mood and the Wife's indifference. For months I knew Carissa's and Rosa's handwriting better than their voices.

At school the habit was hard to break, but we were a lot less careful about it.

In the third or fourth week of Beth's stay at St. Joke's, my English class was canceled and we got shoved into a computer lab with the students that were there working. When I saw Beth was in the class, her hair pulled back in a big gingery poof of curls, my heart beat so hard I felt it behind my eyes, in the palms of my hands. The base of my dick.

One wild, solid thunk of happiness.

Sweat slicked my hands, making some of the cuts

that refused to heal sting, but I barely felt it. That was the power of Beth.

I tried not to grin as I walked down the last aisle to where she was sitting, and like God wanted me there, the computer beside her was empty.

And I was about to ask, *is it cool if I sit here*, when she looked up at me with a smile. I swear, that smile was like nothing I'd ever seen. Like nothing that had ever been flashed my way.

I had a few memories of my mother—a harried whisper, the strong tug of her hand on mine. Picnic lunches on a red blanket and the rumble of her voice as she read me a story. I remembered enough to know she was real young and we lived lean and there'd been scary times. She'd left me alone a lot. Died of an overdose in someone else's apartment and no one came looking for me in ours. I'd been alone for days, until hunger drove me out into the streets.

And she'd been pretty, or maybe every kid feels that way about their mom. I don't know. We didn't talk about moms a lot at St. Joke's. We thought about them constantly but rarely said a word about them.

But I knew I got my blond hair and blue eyes from her, and her smile had made me feel safe.

But that smile was never like this.

Never for me.

I can't tell you what it was like, having someone

after having no one. And that person was so happy I was there, she couldn't contain it, didn't even bother to try. Didn't even care who saw it.

You, that smile said, *make me happy.*

I didn't ask to sit down. I just sat in the spot like it had been left for me.

"What are you doing here?" she whispered and I started to explain but the teacher shushed me fast.

And just as fast Beth opened her notebook and took out her pencil. I grabbed my pencil out of my butt pocket, the eraser long ago chewed off.

Class canceled, I wrote. *Teacher got sick.*

Our teacher is high, she wrote. *Literally.*

I glanced up at the front of the class, and the teacher was organizing the pencil drawer at the top of the desk.

What do you know from high? I asked her, because if there was a straight in this world, it was her.

What don't I know? she wrote.

I laughed before I got a look at her face, her mouth all twisted like she'd eaten something bitter.

You're not joking?

Not joking.

I wanted to ask her a bunch of questions about her mom and where she came from and how she got to St. Joke's, but one thing she'd made clear in the last few weeks—she didn't talk about that shit. Ever.

You sleeping okay? I wrote, and she jerked back, looked at me sideways.

I'm sorry, I wrote. *I heard you last night.*

My mom used to give me these pills to help me sleep, she wrote. *I haven't had them in a while. I can get bad dreams.*

The page was full and I reached forward to turn it but she jerked it out of the way and it fell to the floor, the notebook splitting open on a page with a drawing on it. We both bent to grab it and bonked heads at the same time.

We groaned and laughed, holding our heads where we'd hit each other, and the notebook lay open between us.

"Did you draw that?" I asked her in a whisper. The whole page from end to end was an underwater scene with all these fish hidden in seaweed, and when I looked carefully, there was a squid, and when I looked again, it was gone.

"Yeah," she whispered and grabbed it off the floor, closing it so I couldn't see the picture anymore. "I was just fooling around."

I put my hand over the notebook, my fingers touching the fleshy part of her palm.

She turned my hand over, revealing the ripple of

the cuts from her first night at St. Joke's. The cut near my thumb that kept opening no matter how hard I tried to help it heal.

"Do they still hurt?" she whispered.

I shook my head, unable to speak, my throat like a straw I could not suck any air through.

"I'm sorry," she whispered, and I felt my body get so hot so fast I thought I was going to combust right there.

She touched one of the scars, her finger tracing it from one side of my palm to the other. I closed my eyes in the ecstatic fucking pain of it. I could die, I thought. Right now.

I shifted to keep my books in my lap so she couldn't see my hard-on.

Embarrassed, I wanted to jerk back, but I didn't. I left my hand there. My skin touching hers.

And she left her hand there, her skin touching mine.

THE ADDRESS IN Santa Barbara was on a road along a high ridge above the town. Through the trees I could see the city, all lit up in its grid pattern, and the dark ocean beyond it, broken up only by the oil rigs off the coast.

The houses were built into the ridge, thick trees

behind each house to provide privacy from the road. But the houses that I could see, they were mansions. Big fucking mansions.

And the numbering made no sense.

"Where is 1137," I breathed, peering over the steering wheel as I slowed down to a crawl. "Where the hell?"

I turned a slight curve, and the house in front of me was lit up. Every window was illuminated, and cars were parked on the road and filling the big driveway. I could hear the music from the house inside my car.

Pest sat up and looked out the window.

Pest loved a party, and with me around she didn't get to go to many. All those people to pet her, all that food dropped on the floor. Dog's paradise.

"Sorry, girl," I told her. "You can't come with me."

She gave me her best *suck it, my human* look.

I parked in front of the driveway, boxing in about three other BMWs.

"Here we go," I murmured. I tied my tie, looking at myself in the rearview mirror to confirm I'd made a total hash of it, and I slipped my new ID in my pocket.

When I opened the car door, the music coming from the house was so loud, the bass turned up so high I could feel it in my chest, battling with the pound of my heartbeat. I could hear the roar of voices, too.

This wasn't just any kind of party. That much was

clear.

The front door was surrounded by potted trees, and there were two security cameras trained on me. I ignored both of them and knocked.

I had no idea what I was doing, but I figured acting like I knew what I was doing would at least get me in the door. I hoped. I'd make it up as I went.

The door opened, and a giant man with a severely broken nose and no neck stood staring at me.

Bodyguard. Clearly.

"Who are you?" he asked.

"Driver," I said.

"Can I see some ID?"

I gave him the card Carissa had made for me.

"Who called you?" he asked and I blanked. "Did her mother call you?" he asked.

"No," I said, operating purely on gut instinct. "She did." I had no clue who *she* was. I wanted to ask if she was Beth. But I'd give myself away.

The bodyguard's eyebrows lifted. "No shit?"

"No shit."

"Well good fucking luck to you," he said with a dry, bitter laugh. "I'd have her assistant go find her, but Beth got shit canned earlier. And I'm not leaving this door. You're gonna have to find her yourself."

"Beth?" I said, too sharp 'cause the guy narrowed his eyes at me. "She's the one who ordered the car."

"That makes more sense. She might be getting her stuff. I don't know." He jerked his thumb back into the party. "Go ahead and take a look around."

Oh fuck. Was it possible it was going to be this easy? Pick up Beth and take her to Arizona?

He stood aside and let me pass, and I waded into the wall of people that made up the party. There was a lot of skin. A lot of pretty. The smell of sex and dope thick in the air. There was a song thumping through the house, and I kind of knew it. Mostly didn't.

I kept hearing the name Jada, and I felt like I should know who that was. But I didn't.

As I got out of earshot of the bodyguard at the door, I turned to the closest, soberest person I could find. Not an easy feat as just about everyone was heavy-lidded and wasted. All these people out of control like this made me nervous.

All this skin made me nervous.

The sex.

And I hated that it made me nervous.

"Hey, man," I asked a boy who didn't look old enough to be holding that drink in his hand. "You know where Beth is?"

"Who's Beth?"

"Jada's assistant?" That was a stab in the dark.

The kid shrugged and went back to his conversation. The living room opened up to a huge kitchen filled with more people. Beyond the wall of sliding glass doors was a pool and a deck. Also full of people.

There was so much skin. Girls in bikinis and skirts. Short shorts that looked like bikini bottoms. None of the guys were wearing shirts. Like…none of them.

I tried not to stare, but it just seemed to be everywhere I looked.

So much skin touching other skin. There were couples making out on couches and against walls. One woman was grinding up on another woman against the sliding glass door. In the pool two men were doing something under the water. I didn't know what, but their faces told a pretty raunchy story.

My heart rate went up; my blood thumped in my veins. I didn't know where to look or how to move through this crowd. There was sweat crawling down my back.

I felt like a sixteen-year-old walking into an orgy.

"What's wrong with you, man?" a guy asked when he caught me staring at the girl he was with. She'd taken off her shirt, and her tan lines, the paleness of her breasts against the darkness of her shoulders and arms…

"Sorry," I muttered.

I glanced at my watch. The half hour I'd carved out for this side trip by speeding my way down Highway 1 was mostly gone. I needed to find Beth, figure out what

I was supposed to pick up, and get the fuck out of here so I could hit my window.

"Excuse me," I asked another person, a woman this time, mixing drinks in a blender. She wore a bright green bikini and a pair of sunglasses despite the lack of sun outside.

"Do you know where Beth is?"

"That buzzkill is gone! And good riddance!" She laughed and turned on the blender. The lid wasn't on, and she got splattered with margarita. She and her friends dissolved into laughter.

I kept asking, making my way back farther into the house where the crowd got sparser. The hallway leading to the bedrooms was not nearly as crowded.

"I'm looking for Beth," I said to just about everyone I passed. "Have you seen her?"

A rather harried-looking bald man finally had an answer for me. "Yeah, she was back in the guest room packing up her stuff not too long ago. She said she wasn't leaving until she had a chance to talk to Jada."

Guest bedroom. Excellent.

I shouldered my way down the hall, opening closed doors as I went and shutting them quickly when I found them empty or full of people fooling around.

The third door I opened was empty, but the light by the bed was on and the door on the far side of the bed was open. There was a suitcase on the bed, a heap of clothes sitting in it.

"Beth?" I said. "You here?" I walked around the bed and looked into the en suite. Nothing. Empty.

Shit.

In the hall there was only one more door I hadn't opened. When I tried it, it was locked.

I knocked, rapping my fist against the wood pretty hard so I could be heard above the sounds of the party. The door opened, and a pretty black woman, with swollen eyes from crying, stood there.

"Who are you?" she demanded.

"The driver," I said. "Who are you?"

The girl shook her head, fresh tears in her eyes. "I used to be her assistant—"

"You're Beth?"

"Yeah," she breathed. "She fired me, but I'm not leaving as long as these jerks are here!"

"We heard that!" someone yelled from inside the room.

I pushed open the door, confused as I'd ever been. Because while this pretty woman might be Beth, she was not my Beth.

You don't have a Beth, asshole.

"Did her mom send you?" Beth asked.

"No," I answered. In my world moms weren't really a thing.

We were standing in the small foyer of a giant master bedroom, and I could hear voices beyond the corner so I just kept walking, determined to figure out what the fuck I was supposed to be doing.

The scene on the king-size bed took a second to process. A woman, who appeared already passed out, long dark hair falling over her face, her skirt pushed up above her waist, revealing a pair of black lace panties, was getting an injection in her thigh from a man in a suit. Two other people, a man and a woman, lay sprawled across the bed, watching.

"I told you not to do that!" Beth cried as she rushed past me toward the man in the suit. "She's had enough." As a junkyard dog she was pretty sad. I mean, Pest would have done a better job of barking that man away than she did.

"It's done," the man said, dropping a spent vial and a syringe into a bag on the bedside table. He stood up and peeled off a pair of latex gloves. "And you..." he said, looking at Beth with supreme disdain, "have been fired."

"Yeah, Beth," the man on the bed slurred while slowly easing across the bed to lie spooned with the unconscious woman. "You've been fired."

The guy on the bed ran his hand over the unconscious woman's ass.

"Don't touch her," I snapped, my voice crackling through the room, drawing everyone's attention to me.

I didn't like watching passed-out women getting pawed. It was vile. This whole fucking scene was vile.

And as a junkyard dog, I was completely effective.

"Who are you?" the man who'd had the syringe asked. Fuck, if he was a doctor, he should have that license yanked and fast.

"I'm the driver," I said like I was God. "Who are you?"

"I'm Jada's personal physician, and we didn't order a car," he said and glanced over at the stoned couple. "Did we?"

"Her mother probably," the woman on the bed sneered, giving Beth an evil eye.

"Well, that's a problem," the doctor said.

"Her mother is better than you," Beth said. "And someone needs to know what you're doing to her before she ends up like Michael Jackson."

"Jesus, you are overdramatic," the woman on the bed sighed, rolling her eyes so hard it was a wonder they didn't get lost.

"Jada!" the doctor said, bending down to the passed-out woman. He gave her a hard shove. "Jada!" he yelled in her ear.

"Hey!" I snapped, stepping toward the doctor. Frankly, if he was a legit doctor, I'd eat my fake driver badge. "Don't manhandle her like that."

"Jada!" he yelled again, smacking her.

I shoved the doctor back, getting between him and the woman on the bed. This wasn't my current mission, but there was no way I could just stand back and let this shit happen.

"Touch her again and I'll break your hand."

The doctor held up his hands. "No need to get excited."

"Beth?" I said. "Do the cops need to be called?"

The room was silent. Still. Like this was a line that had never been crossed. Or mentioned. But they all knew it was there.

In my opinion the cops needed to be called yesterday, but then what did I know?

"Beth!" I snapped.

"Y-yes," Beth said. "The cops need to be called."

"Do that, then." I didn't take my eyes off the "doctor."

"You don't know what you're doing," he said in a quiet voice, running a hand over his tie, and I knew a nervous tell when I saw it.

"Is that supposed to scare me?" I asked. "Like I'm the criminal here?"

"Jada," the doctor said, like he was smarter than me and he was doing me a favor by explaining himself, "is in a highly fragile state. She's suffering from depression and exhaustion. She's an insomniac who is experiencing manic episodes. I was called in because her friends are scared she'll take her life."

"Those friends?" I asked, jerking my thumb back at the couple on the bed. They were preoccupied with the powder in lines on the bedside table.

"You know something, *I'm* calling the cops," the doctor said, backing up another step. "You broke in here."

"I was let in." This guy was not going to be calling any fucking cops. "But go ahead. I'm sure those two won't mind. Just let them finish that coke they're hoovering."

"You're threatening me. You're threatening Jada—"

"Who are you kidding, John?" a slow, rough voice said from the bed. "It's bad for all of us if you call the cops."

"Jada!"

I turned to see the dark-haired woman on the bed sitting up. Her clothes were dishevelled, twisted on her body. Her breast was nearly revealed through the neck hole; her skirt was still hiked up around her waist. She fumbled with the clothes, but then stopped like it was just too hard.

Her hair was not all black—it had green, blue, purple, and pink highlights. It was beautiful, like an oil spill. Well, like a beautiful oil spill. She pushed her long hair off her face, and I nearly died. Right there. Cardiac arrest.

It was Beth sitting there.

My Beth.

8

Tommy

INSTINCT KICKED IN, and I stepped back. Looked away.

I had to get out of that room. I had to turn around and walk right out of this place. Away from her. Away from what she needed.

Beth. And she needed help.

I wasn't that guy anymore, the kid trying to take care of everyone and fucking it up. I didn't have the strength for that. The will.

I wasn't that kid, and I couldn't save anyone. I'd barely saved myself.

Least of all Beth.

I tried that already.

Fuck you, Bates, I thought.

I took another step back. Another. I'd go down for the cop-killing crime. Fine. I'd been resigned to jail a long time ago.

"Who are you?" she said. And I knew without looking that she was talking to me. The rough rasp of her voice forced my feet to a stop on the thick carpet. I remembered that voice. I didn't want to, but I did.

Because it still sounded like my life. Gritty and raw. Rough and dark.

It sounded like the happiest three months of my life.

Beth.

I closed my eyes.

I was a shit hero; I knew that. But somehow I could never stop myself from trying.

When I opened my eyes and looked at her it was an act of will not to see her as the girl in pigtails I'd loved so hard. I had to actively *not* remember her. Not pull out all those memories and attach them to her, like ornaments off a Christmas tree.

Her eyes when she looked at me had no recognition. I was a stranger to her. It wasn't a surprise considering the state she was in, and our past wasn't something that needed to be talked about here. But I found myself wanting to answer her.

I'm Tommy. Remember? When we were kids? I was your friend. Or maybe you were mine. Or maybe I imagined all that. But we knew each other. We did.

And that's what Bates was counting on. That was the trap he'd laid for me. Why he knew I'd make good on my promise.

Because I'd loved this girl once. And failing her was my great regret.

"The driver," I said in a quiet voice. She kept looking at me, and I crouched down so she could see me better. The freckles were still there, those beautiful constellations, that one-of-a-kind artwork. My fingers twitched with the urge to touch them, connect them across her chin and neck. The one at the top of her lip.

That one had been my favorite. I'd studied it. Tasted it.

Her amber gaze made tracks all over my face, and I waited, my breath half held, for her to recognize me. To see in the man I'd become, the boy I'd been.

"Do I know you?" she asked, stoned and confused.

"No," I lied. Or maybe it was the truth. I couldn't say.

"Did you call a driver, Jada?" the "doctor" asked.

Her face creased. "I don't know. Did I?"

"Jada," the doctor said. "I'm having this man arrested—"

Beth, the assistant, came back in the door, looking defiant and terrified all at once. "I've called the police. I gave them your name and told them you were here operating with a fake license."

"Shit," the doctor muttered and started packing up his things, his bluff called. All his concern for Jada was clearly secondary to his fear of the police.

"What a piece of shit you are," I said to him.

"Fuck you," he said. "Like you know anything. Jada, honey. I'll be in touch."

And like that the doctor was gone, Beth, at the door, all but hissing at him as he left. A better junkyard cat than dog.

"Get lost," I said to the couple on the bed, who'd been watching everything with wide eyes.

Without another word they snorted up the last of the coke, got up, and stumbled out after the doctor.

"I'm going to go let security know police are coming," Beth said. "Don't… don't leave her."

"I won't."

Beth vanished, and I turned back to Jada, who sat there, a little slumped, watching me. Her eyes were startling.

So familiar and so different at the same time.

Her hair slipped over her shoulders, down across her eyes, and my fingers twitched to push it back, to stroke it off her shoulders with my palms, to hold it in my fist at the nape of her neck.

I'd never seen her hair down. Except for that one time. That horrible time.

When we were kids, her hair had been red. I'd never seen a light-skinned black girl with red hair and freckles before, and she told me it was a mutation in the MC1R gene. How I remembered that, I couldn't say. Except that I remembered everything she told me. Like those three months with her were crystallized. Solid moments I'd taken out over the years and watched like movies. Until I forced myself to stop. To give them up.

Because what was the point? Up until this moment, she'd been gone. So gone it was like I'd dreamed her. Made her up.

I could see freckles on her chest, the inside of her arm. Hidden away. Secret.

They made me breathless.

She smiled at me, dazed. "I know you."

"You don't," I said. Because I couldn't do this if she did. If we had to remember who we'd been to each other.

She wrinkled her nose, and my heart squeezed so hard I saw stars.

When she stood, she was a breath away, her hand on my wrist.

"You're…really good-looking."

I felt myself smile. She could always do that—make me smile when I'd rather not.

"Oh," she breathed and touched the dimple in my cheek. "Will you look at that? A dimple. Did you know you had a dimple?"

"I'm aware." Now I couldn't *stop* smiling.

"I'd like to kiss you." She'd said that same thing to me a million years ago. Announced it, because she'd been that kind of person—full of intention and courage. Bold. She'd been bold.

And I wanted to fucking roll in that boldness. Soak it into my dried-out skin.

"You should be kissed," she said. "You got a mouth that wants it. Do you want to be kissed?"

God, I did. I wanted her to put her lips on me and her tongue in my mouth and I wanted to taste her, to see if she still tasted like Skittles. If the grown-up woman liked what the teenage girl had loved so much.

Fuck, I wanted everything we never did. Everything I'd dreamed of. Everything I didn't even know to dream about.

But she was fucked-up and in some kind of trouble, and I was in my own, and the whole world was a little upside down.

I stepped back, and she bent forward, off-balance without me there to hold her up with my dimple.

She grabbed my elbow, blew out a breath. Seemed to crumple before me.

"Jada?" Not Beth. This whole thing would be easier if she wasn't Beth and I wasn't Tommy and we were strangers to each other.

"I want to leave," she said.

I heaved a sigh of relief, blinked with surprise. "Are

you sure?"

She nodded. "I can't do this anymore."

It was such a loaded statement. Such a sad sentence. Her knees buckled and she collapsed toward me and I caught her in my arms. "Jada?" I whispered, trying not to feel the skin of her arms. The lace of her hair. "Are you okay?"

"Get me out of here." Her voice was sleepy and slurred. Whatever that shot was that she'd been given was kicking in.

Chaos broke out in the other part of the house, and I scooped Jada up in my arms. She was barely conscious and featherlight. So light it made my heart ache. So light it left bruises in places I thought too hard and callused for such things. Her chest rose and fell with her breathing, and I could see the pulse working in her neck. A steady beat.

She was warm against me. Alive and flush—and I ignored all of it. I shrank back in my body so I didn't feel a goddamned thing.

I wasn't thinking. This thing I was doing was long past thinking. This was some instinct shit happening inside of me. This felt nearly outside of my control.

And it also felt really familiar.

I should call Simon, I thought, *let him talk some reason into me.*

But I didn't.

There were sliding glass doors on the other side of the bedroom. The deck outside was dark and unoccupied. With one hand I opened the doors and stepped out into the cool night air. I walked along the side of the house, away from the party, until I got to the driveway and my car, sitting there with my dog in it.

Through the glass of the passenger window I watched Pest freaking out at the sight of me.

In the distance I heard the beginning wail of a police siren.

The front doors opened, and people were flooding out.

I fished the key out of my pocket and hit the button opening the doors and laid Jada carefully on her side in the backseat. And then I ran around to the driver's seat and I drove away from that party and the cops as fast as I could. Pest climbed from the front seat into the back, to lie curled up on the floorboards beside Jada.

"Good girl," I said to Pest, wiping away the cold sweat pouring down my face.

I avoided the coastal highway, zigzagging through the mountains and then the desert on smaller roads, feeling every minute like I was about to get pulled over. But behind me was only empty highway, not a cop in sight.

The envelope with all my ID and the scrap of paper was on the passenger seat, crinkled slightly from Pest lying on it. One eye on the road, I fished out my phone from my pocket and called the cell phone number written there.

It didn't ring. It went right to a robot voice saying, "Leave a message."

"Carissa," I sighed, my voice low so I didn't wake up Jada in the backseat. "This is Tommy. What... I have..." Her name stuck in my throat. "Beth...I mean, Jada. Am I supposed to have her? Is she the thing I'm supposed to be dropping off? What the fuck have you set me up for?"

I mean, what were the chances that I was supposed to actually kidnap a pop star?

Low. The chances were really fucking low that was what I was supposed to do. So not only did I have to worry about cops, but I had to worry about Bates on my goddamned tail because I'd screwed this up.

"Call me back."

I hung up and tossed the phone in the passenger seat. In the rearview mirror I had a good look at Jada, making sure she was still breathing. She was, her chest rising and falling under the paper-thin white T-shirt.

Fuck. What was I doing?

My phone buzzed with an incoming text, and I grabbed it.

All is according to plan, read the text from the phone number I just dialed. *Continue to drop-off.*

So the plan was taking Jada? I'd acted on some kind of instinct, needing to get her out of that shitty environment where everyone was taking advantage of her and the only person that seemed to care had just been fired.

But that had been the plan all along? The highway in front of me was empty, the moon a big white slice out of a dark purple sky.

What about cops? I texted.

Avoid them, was texted back.

"Fuck," I breathed.

Yeah. Avoid the cops, because the biggest pop sensation in the world right now was in my backseat.

And I just kidnapped her.

9

Jada

UGH.

Shit.

I mean…

I couldn't even finish that thought.

My body was floating. And humming and my head was expanding with every heartbeat like a balloon being blown up too big.

Don't pop, I told my head. *Don't pop. I still need you.*

This new thing Dr. John was giving me to help me sleep…it was bad. I mean, it was great in that it turned off my brain enough that I slept, which was a miracle.

But it made me wake up like a stranger. Like I had no idea who I was.

I was twenty percent myself. Eighty percent someone else. Someone I didn't like a whole bunch. I didn't even hear music anymore. And my hands, when I held the airbrush… they didn't know what to do.

It was too much. I would tell Dr. John that. He would listen; he wasn't like my mother. I was paying him to do what I asked. Jesus, I couldn't lift my eyelids. Or my head. I was a thousand pounds. How was I supposed to go onstage like this?

Oh, that's right, I wasn't. It was over.

A dark and awful queasiness rippled through me. Something that felt like failure. Or regret. The North American tour was done and Europe was supposed to begin and I didn't...I didn't know how to do it. How to keep going. I wanted—in my dark, tiny heart—to stop.

That's how Dr. John got hired two weeks ago in the first place. He was supposed to wind me up like a doll and send me dancing off onto the stage. His pills and syringes took care of the anxiety that crept up and followed me like a shadow, the fear that made me cling to my dressing room chair, wishing I'd never started any of this.

And then, when I got offstage, he gave me the nighty-night shot.

The nighty-night shot was a real problem.

Who was I kidding? All of it was a problem.

But this life... this pop-star thing? It was so much harder than I'd thought it would be.

Something cold brushed my hand, and the very distinct smell of dog washed over me.

"Beth?" I said, but it came out of my dry throat like

a whimper.

The dog nosed me again and his tongue licked my face and with my eyes closed I stretched out a hand and found the dog's back. I burrowed my fingers into its thick fur until I felt the warmth of its skin.

I'd wanted a dog, but everyone told me it didn't make any sense on the road. Except my assistant, Beth. Beth told me I should get one. Beth told me I needed something to take care of.

Something rattled in the back of my brain about my assistant, some low-level anxiety slipping over me. *What did I do to Beth?*

Funny that my assistant's name was also my name. I felt like I was talking about myself in the third person half the time. The dark irony of asking *what did I do to Beth?* was not lost on me. It could in fact be the name of my autobiography. My juicy tell-all.

CliffNotes version: I killed Beth. That girl I'd been. The patient, waiting victim. So good, that girl. So dumb. Terrified of being wrong. Terrified of…everything, really. Beth had been useless, so I became Jada.

Jada was fucking fierce. Jada wasn't scared of shit. No one—absolutely no one—hurt Jada.

I loved Jada.

I opened my eyes and stared into the face of…*Jesus.* Was that a dog? It looked like a rat. Or a squirrel. Its tongue came out and licked its own nose, its long tooth hanging out of its jaw.

Did I really get a dog? Did I, in fact, get the ugliest dog in the world? Someone should stop me from doing that kind of thing. I couldn't take care of a dog. I could barely take care of myself.

Assistant Beth would have to take the creature back where it came from.

"You stink," I said to the dog, though no sound came out. I closed my eyes again. God, I was thirsty. So, fucking thirsty.

"Can someone get me a drink?" I croaked. "Anyone?"

Silence. Nothing but silence. Maybe everyone was in the other room? Which was weird. There were people with me…always. Like in bed with me. In the bathroom with me. Half the time I didn't know their names or how they came to be peeing while I took a shower—but it seemed to be part of this life I'd picked.

Like by choosing door number two—international fame—I also picked a group of nameless people who just constantly milled around me. I hadn't been alone in months.

I loved it. What a relief it was, that break from all my solitude.

"Come on!" I barked, the sound more like a pitiful gasp. "Someone!"

No one.

I opened my eyes again, the world slowly coming into focus.

It wasn't whatever was in Dr. John's syringe making me feel like I was moving.

I was moving in the backseat of a car.

And I was alone back here. Just me and the dog, the black leather beneath me warm from my body heat. I'd been here awhile.

"Hey!" I yelled. "What's…what's going on?"

The driver didn't answer, and I realized I was barely audible, my throat all swollen and pinched. My head was pounding.

I slowly sat up, my hand over my eyes keeping out the sunlight. "Where are we going?"

"We're almost there," a deep voice said. "Why don't you go back to sleep?"

"We're almost where?" I asked.

He rattled off some address that meant nothing to me.

"Where's Beth?" I asked.

"Your assistant?"

I groaned. "Yes, my assistant." Who was this driver? Some new guy?

"You don't remember?" he asked, and I sensed a little bit of judgment in his voice. And man, nothing got to me like judgment.

"Fuck you, man," I snapped. "You're just the *driver.*"

Was I a hypocrite fighting judgment with judgment? Yes. The guy probably had a screenplay or a fitness YouTube channel. No one was just one thing.

"Sorry," I said. Apologizing was an old habit I couldn't quite break.

"Me too," he said.

Look at us playing nice.

I looked around for my phone, checked my pockets. Realized not only did I not have a phone, I didn't have my purse. Or shoes.

"What the hell?" I muttered. I shifted around until I saw the driver in the rearview mirror.

Shit. He was big. Really big. Huge shoulders, big wide chest in a white dress shirt. He had a black tie pulled loose around his neck. But despite that tie and the dress shirt, he looked like a thug. He had a neck, sort of. And his nose had been broken a few times too many. He had a weird crackling energy around him. Still…but not. Calm…but not. Like he was waiting.

And he was a total stranger.

I'd been using the same driver for like the last few months. The record company had been paying for him.

A chill ran across my scalp.

Somehow my mother had found me, she'd broken through all the disillusionment charms and spells I'd cast around my life (Harry Potter references, another old habit I couldn't break) and gotten in touch with my people, who'd gotten her in touch with me. I had no idea how it happened, how she tracked me down after all these years. Maybe she'd recognized me somehow in the footage of my spectacular disaster at the Hollywood Bowl the other night. I had no clue. And it didn't even matter.

All that mattered was that she'd found me.

And now she was making noises about seeing me. Having me evaluated. Putting me under her care again.

All things she could do. Only because she'd proven all along that there was very little she couldn't do. Not when it came to me. And now, after that thing onstage, I'd blown the one advantage I had over my mother—my own credibility.

"Did my mom send you?" I asked, my brain clearing in a hurry.

"No," he said. "I have nothing to do with your mom."

I wasn't sure I believed him, and I shifted a little bit more, wincing when my skin peeled off the leather. Finally I got a look at the man's face.

He had blue eyes and pale blond hair, cut short. He was...very handsome. The way real people were handsome. With flaws and imperfections that told a story. I'd spent the last few months with people who worked hard to get rid of those imperfections. Who looked good in a completely perfect way.

It was creepy.

But he wore that scar on his chin and the healed-over piercings in his ear and his chapped lips, his badly broken nose—he wore them well. And the story those things told was a rough one.

Outlaw.

His eyes were narrowed against the sun coming through the windshield, and when he winced, flipping down the visor—though it did little good—in the corner of his mouth, right there in his cheek, he had a dimple.

I sucked in a breath. Held it. Couldn't let it go.

Did I know him? I knew him? Everything in my body screamed that I knew him.

And that he was…dangerous. Dangerous to me somehow. A threat.

And not just because I didn't know who he was and I was in the backseat of his car.

There was something worse. I just couldn't re-member it.

My stomach went cold, my belly full of fear, and the rush of adrenaline cleared whatever drugs lingered in my system.

This…this wasn't right.

How did I not remember getting in a car?

I had to fire Dr. John. Had to. Beth had been right; he was a total mistake. I'd let shit get out of hand.

"Who are you?" I asked.

He glanced at me for a long time in the rearview mirror, like maybe I was supposed to know him.

"My name is Sam," he finally said.

"You have ID, Sam?"

He tossed back a driver's license and a license for an agency. They bounced off my leg and landed faceup on the seat beside me. Sam Johnson.

Seemed legit.

But…not.

The dog in front of me whined in its throat as if the thing could tell I was freaking out.

"Why do you have a dog?" I asked.

"Come here, Pest," the driver said, and just like that the tiny little rat dog tried to climb up over the middle console.

"Can you give her a boost?" the guy asked, and I gave the dog a little shove up and over the middle console and she tumbled into the passenger seat. *What is going on?* "That better?" the man asked, and I met his gaze in the rearview mirror. I didn't want to, but I didn't seem to have a choice. Those eyes were magnetic. And familiar?

"Sorry if she was bothering you."

"What kind of driver brings their dog?"

"She's a working dog."

"Are you blind?" Sarcasm was my lifeboat in a storm.

"Social anxiety." The curl of his lip said that he got the joke.

"Whatever," I muttered, looking out the window, refusing to acknowledge the humor. "Where are we?"

"Arizona."

"Why?"

He was silent for a long time and then shrugged. "You called me, Jada."

"I gave you the address?"

He nodded.

I didn't know anything about anything in Arizona. Except there were fancy spas in Arizona. And I'd been spending time with the kinds of people who went to fancy spas in Arizona. Had I decided at some point last night that what I needed was to get away from everyone and everything and eat some organic salmon and sit in some mud? Maybe get myself off some of the shit Dr. John was giving me?

That sounded like an excellent idea. I hoped last-night me did exactly that. It would be a relief to actually go ahead and believe that. But I couldn't.

My mom was in the picture again, and I couldn't trust anything.

"Can I use your phone?"

"For what?"

"To call someone." Beth would be freaking out; we didn't go a day without talking. Barely went three hours without talking. "I don't have my phone." Or my purse. Or my shoes.

Why would I leave without my stuff? My laptop? I didn't go anywhere without my laptop.

"I can't…I can't do that," he said.

"What? Why?"

"We're on a time frame," he said. "I can't have you throwing off the time frame."

That reeked of bullshit.

"I'm paying you, aren't I? It's my time frame. Give me your goddamn phone."

"Nope."

Was I being…*kidnapped?* I mean, I had no experience with that. Katy Perry told me a story once that scared the bejesus out of me, but so far none of my fans had gotten too weird.

This felt weird. Really weird.

I sprang up from the seat, and it must have been too fast, because my head went all swimmy and my stomach tried to crawl up my throat.

The nighty-night shot was a real problem in the morning.

"Are you okay?" he asked, his eyes pinning me to the seat through the rearview mirror. That was some potent eye contact.

"I think… I'm going to be sick."

And just like that Sam, my potential kidnapper, pulled over to the side of the road, gravel crunching under the wheels of the car. The car was barely in park before I had the door popped open. The fresh air cleared my head enough that I was pretty sure I wasn't going to puke.

We were surrounded by the high desert, nothing but dirt and cactus and scrub for miles. The breeze that blew in smelled hot and sandy.

It certainly looked like Arizona.

Sam opened the front door of the car and came to stand in my open door. I looked up, closing one eye as the sun gave him a halo effect around his head and blinded me. I tried—I really did try not to notice how solid he was. How lean and thick at the same time. I imagined under that coffee-stained shirt, he was all muscle.

He didn't look like a driver. At all.

"Are you kidnapping me, Sam?" I asked. He opened his mouth to answer, to no doubt say something about being a driver or just following my orders, but this whole thing felt wrong. "And cut the bullshit."

"Kidnapping," he finally said, like he was really sorry about it, "is a really strong word."

I sucked in air, my head reeling.

Shit. Shitshitshitshit.

"If it makes you feel any better, you said you wanted to leave that house."

"No, Sam, it doesn't make me feel better. Did you happen to notice I was out of my mind at the time?"

He nodded. His ears were red and I realized maybe coming at my kidnapper with my claws extended was not the best call.

"Are you… are you a fan?" I tried to smile, to make this normal. I mean, I watched *Nashville*; I knew the script.

"No," he said with a dry laugh. "I'm sorry to say, I am not."

Shit. That wasn't in the script.

"Are you doing this for money?" I asked. "Because whatever you're being paid… I can double it. Triple it." That was unlikely. For being one of the biggest names in music at the moment, I had no money. Not real money. I had money my manager gave me like an allowance. Or he paid for things—like Dr. John and food. Parties. Drugs.

Beth was sure I was getting ripped off.

"I'm doing this because I don't have a choice," he said.

"Everyone has a choice." I tried to smile, but it didn't feel convincing. Not having a choice was something I understood.

Some people just had choices taken from them.

Some gave them away.

Some didn't even know what choice looked like.

And I'd been all three of those people at different parts of my life.

"Do you remember me?" he asked like if I remembered him, this would all make sense.

"Yes, you're Sam the Driver." *Slash kidnapper.*

But he wasn't. It was obvious. There was something so much bigger going on.

Oh God, what was I supposed to say? About a million times in the last seven months I'd wished there was some kind of handbook for this life I'd been thrust into. And this, dealing with crazy, kidnapping non-fans—it would be nice to know what to do.

"You don't remember me," he said, his voice not sad or mad or anything.

"I'm sorry."

"Don't be." He smiled, just a little, with like one-quarter of his mouth. The dimple flickered but didn't commit. "It's better that way."

"I can tell."

The air cleared my head, and I took giant breaths of it, stalling while trying to figure out what to do.

The car was still running.

Before I'd fully thought it out, I was over the console and into the front seat. I had one foot on the gas and my hand on the gear shift when my lap was suddenly full of dog. Or rat or whatever. She had her paws on my shoulders, her snaggletooth practically in my face.

I was stunned.

And that stunned moment was all my kidnapper needed to reach in the open door of the front seat and take the key out of the ignition.

"Pest," he said. "Scoot."

The dog licked me before jumping over to the passenger seat. Kidnapper crouched down in the open door, and I couldn't look at him—I was about to cry and I wouldn't be giving him that kind of satisfaction.

"Why are you doing this?" I asked, hating that my voice shook.

"It's… it's a long story. Beth—"

He stopped. I stilled. Chills ran down my arms. Across my whole body.

No one called me Beth. No one had in a long time. I wasn't Beth anymore. Hadn't been for years. Legally and everything.

"How do you know my name?"

"I'm sorry," he said. "I…it was an accident."

"Bullshit!" I cried, looking at him, feeling wild and at the edge of something. Something I didn't want to be at the edge of.

I could only take him in in half glances. Tiny glances. The dimple. The sky-blue color of his eyes. His broad shoulders under that white shirt. He filled up the space of the open car door, and I didn't stand a chance against his size. I couldn't push him or shove him or hurt him.

He could swat me down like a fly.

I couldn't even win against his dog.

And he knew my name. My real name.

"I promise you," he said. "You will not be hurt."

He reached for my face as if to wipe away a tear, and I flinched so hard I hit my head against the headrest, knocked my elbow into the dog, who barked.

"Don't—" I had my hand up like there was a chance I could stop him.

"I'm sorry," he said. "I shouldn't… I'm…sorry."

Kidnapper was easing back, and I took the moment and shoved him as hard as I could, throwing him off-balance enough that he fell to the ground on his ass. I put one bare foot against the door frame and launched myself out of the car.

It was dawn, so the asphalt wasn't hot as I ran across the road for the desert and scrub grass beyond it. There was barbed wire and probably snakes and tons of other shit that could take me down and ruin my escape. But it was this or stay a prisoner, and I'd been a prisoner before.

I'd been a prisoner most of my goddamned life.

No way was I doing that again.

I ran as balls-out as I could, the gravel biting into the bottoms of my feet. I'd hit the gulley beside the road when he yelled:

"Stop. Jesus. Beth!"

I felt him there, just behind me. His heat and his size and then his hand on my shoulder and he was yanking me around, grabbing me. He had my arms pinned against my sides so I couldn't hit him, but I screamed and kicked and tried to head butt him. When that didn't work, I leaned forward and, swallowing my revulsion, sank my teeth into his shoulder. I bit as hard as I could and he swore a blue streak but he didn't let me go. He crossed the road back to the car and practically threw me in the backseat.

"Pest," he said, and the dog was suddenly there like my prison warden.

Kidnapper stood up and looked at the bite I'd given him, his body in the way of any escape I might make.

"Jesus," he yelled. "You fucking bit me."

"I'll do it again, asshole."

"I don't fucking doubt it. What are you thinking, running off like that? You don't have any shoes!"

I blinked, disoriented by his concern about my shoes. But only for a minute.

"Whose fault is that?" I yelled.

"Mine," he said. "It's mine."

The futility of all of this washed over me. I was strung out and suddenly starving, and I didn't have any goddamned shoes.

"I don't know why you're doing this." I was furious and near tears and at the end of whatever rope I used to have.

"Neither do I. I'm sorry. I really am."

"You're working for someone?"

"Sort of."

My heart rate spiked, and adrenaline cleared my head. I'd bite him, I'd beat him, whatever I needed to do to stay away from the only person I knew who would go to this kind of trouble to get me back in their life. "You are working for my mother!"

"I'm not," he said. "I swear on Pest's life that I'm not."

"What's your name? Your real name."

"Does it matter?"

"Well, in my head I'm calling you the Kidnapper, so if you're okay with that?"

"Tom," he said and took a deep breath. "My friends call me Tommy."

Tommy.

That name. The dimples…

It was like my heart stopped. It was like the earth stopped.

I pushed my hair out of my eyes and looked at him.

Really looked at him. And he looked back at me like he knew what was happening in my head. My body.

I knew a Tommy once. A long time ago.

He'd changed me. Changed everything.

But this guy…he didn't look like the boy I'd known.

He looked like the boy I'd known, all grown-up and fed and cared for.

He was Tommy magnified.

"No," I said. Shaking my head, denying the truth even as it stared me in the face with its blue Viking eyes. "That's… you're impossible."

"I'm sorry. I really…I'm sorry."

Tommy had been skinny and tall. All bones over taut white skin. This man was a giant.

"Oh my God…" I breathed, all the memories I'd shoved behind doors and under beds spilling out from their hiding places. "Tommy?"

10

Beth

MY MOM TOOK me to a hypnotherapist after St. Joke's. She said she wanted me to shed light on all the memories, to bring them out into the open so they couldn't fester. We needed to talk, she told me. We needed to process.

I wasn't entirely sure what she needed to process as she hadn't been there, but I didn't put up a fight when she took me to this doctor's office with this big leather couch and a fire in the fireplace, and when he said to relax all my muscles one at a time starting at my feet – I did the opposite.

I tightened. I clenched. I became hard and solid and impenetrable.

I made myself my own armor. And it hurt. And it ached.

But it kept me safe.

Because I knew after Tommy, I couldn't expect another Tommy. There was only one. Which meant I had to protect myself.

The hypnotherapist told my mom after one week that I wasn't a good candidate for hypnosis. And Mom took that as a challenge. Shit got real after that, but the armor only got thicker. Stronger.

It had kept me safe from a lot of shit.

But now… right now…it was gone. And I was all weakness and soft underbelly. I was memory and grief and a longing that hurt.

I tried to be strong, clinging to my Jada persona, but she vanished with the shock.

I was fucking Beth.

And in front of me was the only person I'd ever loved.

"Look at you," I breathed, feeling myself smile.

A smile crossed his face, and it was so familiar, so beloved, tears filled my eyes.

"Someone fed you." He nodded, and my gaze ran laps around his body, over and over again, looking for pieces I'd missed. "You're a man."

"You're a…" he almost said woman, I knew it, in that way I'd always been able to know what he was thinking, but he swallowed the word down and instead said: "singer. An artist. I knew…I knew you'd be something amazing."

I nearly laughed. I was far from amazing.

How could I forget those eyes? I'd taken one look at

them and fallen so hard and so fast it was like I'd become a different person. Someone I didn't recognize. Someone I'd never been before. Confident and funny. Alive, all the way down to the ends of my hair.

The foster home had been a horror show, but somehow...I'd found myself there. I'd found happiness. A kind of innocent desire, a healthy lust.

When I found Tommy.

Was it possible to forget the person you first really revealed yourself to? Or did he just get woven into my skin? My hair? Part of the person I became and every costume I wore after that?

Tommy.

He crouched in the open doorway, blocking the new light of the sun.

"Are you hurt?" he asked. "Your feet?"

My feet could be bleeding. They could be *missing* and I wouldn't feel it.

I had a thousand questions. Important ones about why I was in this car and what he'd been doing the last seven years and did he think about me. Did he miss me?

Like I'd missed him?

But instead I said—stupidly—"I thought you hated dogs?"

It was what he'd said years ago, during one of those long conversations at school. When we couldn't learn enough about each other.

"Dogs or cats?" I'd asked.

"Neither," he'd said. "I don't want another thing to worry about."

His smile, crooked and patchwork with the dimple and the chapped lips—it made me suck in a breath.

"Pest is barely a dog."

I remembered, in a sudden full-body memory, the second he and Simon and Carissa came through that office door seven years ago. I'd been fighting the Pastor with all my strength, and in that second, when they burst in, I stopped fighting. Every muscle went soft. Every fist relaxed.

I gave up and nearly blacked out from the relief.

The exact opposite of the hypnotherapist.

Tommy would take care of me, I'd thought.

It was the first time I ever thought that about any-one.

And the last.

And I wanted to hug him. I wanted to pull him as close as I could to my body. I wanted to hold him in the cradle of my legs and rub my hands over his hair and let him kiss my freckles. I wanted to be that girl. And I wanted him to be that boy. And for a moment, just a moment, this wasn't a kidnapping.

It was a fairy tale.

"Tommy," I breathed. "You're here. I never... I

never thought I'd see you again." And I reached for him. For his face. Beautiful and familiar.

But his smile vanished and he jerked back, away from my touch.

"Don't—" he said and turned away, his ears bright red.

"Don't what?"

He swallowed.

"Touch you?" I asked, my voice strained and tight.

"Remember," he said.

"Don't remember you? Are you joking?"

"Don't think about the past," he said. "I'm not. This is just…this is a job. That's all."

Once upon a time we'd jeopardized everything to touch each other, and now… I didn't even understand what he was saying. Don't *remember*? Was he crazy?

How was this happening? After all these years?

Oh, that's right, because fairy tales weren't real. They were tricks played on girls like Beth. To keep us quiet and calm, to preoccupy us with dreams of boys and rescue so we wouldn't get on our feet and rescue ourselves.

And the boy I'd known had grown up to be a man who could take unconscious women out of their homes without shoes, or ID or phones.

I smacked him. I smacked Tommy so hard it sounded like a gunshot. I smacked him so hard we both jerked back.

I swallowed my apology, cupping my stinging palm in my hand. His face was turning red.

"You're…*kidnapping* me, Tommy?"

"I am."

"You get that this is ridiculous, right?"

"I do."

"So how about you explain it to me!"

He glanced at his watch. "I will, I just… We need to get going, Beth," he said.

Every second of my life since I left him had been about turning myself into something he wouldn't recognize. Something I wouldn't recognize. Burying that real and true part of myself I'd shown him so deep, so far, I never saw it again.

And no one else did either.

I had to be Jada.

Jada was the only way I survived.

"My name is Jada," I said out of sheer habit. Sheer self-protective habit.

"Jada," he said with a nod as if committing it to memory. As if erasing all he could of Beth.

It wasn't a bad idea. I'd done it, too. In fact, I would do it with him. I'd put Jada in charge of shit again.

"I'm sorry," he said.

"Then don't do this. Let me go."

"I can't."

"Well then, what are you waiting for, Tommy? You're in the middle of a kidnapping! You've got a time frame to keep. Chop chop, my friend." Sarcasm was a comfortable place to be. Sarcasm was all Jada. Beth had been too soft for sarcasm.

Tommy shut the door and then locked it with the key fob he'd taken when I tried to drive away.

I rolled my eyes at him in the rearview mirror, but I liked that I was a problem.

Really, was there anything worse than a passive kidnapping victim?

We pulled away from the side of the road, and I exhaled slowly. My brain was chasing itself in circles. I was half here, half in the past.

Concentrate. Concentrate on now. The past is nothing.

"Is this for money?" I asked.

He shook his head.

"You said it's a job."

"Not for money."

"What kind of job isn't for money?"

He didn't answer.

"Is this some kind of Jimmy Fallon prank?" *Please let it be a Jimmy Fallon prank.*

His eyes met mine in the rearview mirror, and I felt the blast of something...sizzly. An echo of that prickly new-love feeling, with all the heat we'd had. God. So much heat. I'd been on fire at the thought of him. My hands—at every available moment—in my panties.

Once this guy showed me what hands down panties could feel like.

None of that, however, is relevant to the fact that he is kidnapping me.

"No. It's not a prank."

"Is it a sex thing?"

His eyes in the mirror were horrified.

"Is it? You've kidnapped me in order to do what we didn't do when we were kids. You looking for a little sexual closure, Tommy? You want me to put my hair up in pigtails and we can find the nearest art room and finish what we started?"

That I was actually trotting out one of my old, post-St. Joke's fantasies shouldn't have been exciting. None of this was…exciting.

But it was. Kind of.

And when his eyes met mine in the mirror—that was exciting too.

"No," he said. And if that was true, fine, but now the idea was here, between us. Like his ugly fucking dog.

We used to want each other so bad I rubbed myself raw in bathrooms in that high school. I'd get worked up just from a glance at his wrist, with its knobby bones and all that promise of manhood. The sound of his voice cutting through the noise of the cafeteria had the power to stop my heart. Turn me to goo.

I'd been a radio with one frequency. Him.

"Then you better start explaining," I said, snapping through the smoky heat in my blood.

"Do you… you remember the foster home?"

I laughed. "Yeah, Tommy," I said with enough sarcasm for, like, twenty kidnap victims. Using up all the sarcasm in a twenty-mile radius. They were running out of it in the Grand Canyon. There would probably be a national shortage. "I remember St. Joke's."

His ears got red, which meant he was blushing, and I hated that I knew that. That those memories lingered like ghosts. "Some people would want to forget what happened there," he said in a low murmur.

I stared at the back of his head, my heart in a knot.

Yeah, I wanted to say. *Some of it was shit but…there was you. There was us.*

And those memories were so sweet. So fine. Worn smooth like pebbles, because I took them out like gems and held them in sweaty, clutching fingers when I needed to remember a time I'd been loved.

There was no way I could have forgotten him. Tommy was too big a memory to forget. Too beautiful a sound to let go of. Despite everything else, there was no forgetting Tommy.

"Is that what you did?" I asked him. *Did you put me in a box and forget me?*

"I tried," he said. And it didn't just hurt; it fucking infuriated me. It filled me with something dark and hollow and hungry. I'd been shining memories of him to a high polish, imagining what would have happened between us if we'd only been regular kids, if Mr. Abrahams hadn't walked in on us.

I'd thought myself so in love that when I finally got away from my mother—I looked for his family.

Looked. For. His. Family.

I'd tried to connect myself to every single part of him I could find. I'd thought I could fix things for him. Or something…

And he'd been trying to forget me?

I called bullshit on that, right there. Something in the way his eyes tracked me in the backseat, the way the tips of his ears were red and his hands were squeezing on that steering wheel told me a different kind of story.

"And yet, here you are, kidnapping me? I don't think it worked, Tommy."

"No," he said in his serious, quiet voice that I remembered so clearly. "It didn't work."

Outside, a dark bird took flight against the peach dawn, and in the silence of the car, the memories sprang up like dandelions in May. Unstoppable.

The art room. The notes under salt shakers. Sitting beside him at church, the distance between our legs delicious and awful at the same time. My nerves still remembered. The wild zing of something so wanted and so forbidden, it left its imprint on my thigh. A tattoo of desire.

The graham crackers.

The fucking graham crackers really started everything.

"You hungry or anything?" he asked like he'd been remembering the crackers too.

I was starving, but I wasn't asking this guy... *my God, Tommy...* for shit. That was how Stockholm syndrome began.

"I'm fine," I said. "Finish your story about how you came to carry me out of a house without shoes, phone or...what else, oh, that's right...consent."

God, I loved Jada.

"You asked me to get you out of there, Jada," he said.

Of course I did.

"Is that making you feel better about this? Or did you happen to notice I was wasted at the time?"

His silence was pretty damning.

"It's a long story," he said with a sigh that told me he'd rather do anything but explain why he had me in the backseat of his car.

"Yeah? Good thing we're on this thousand-mile road trip, isn't it?"

He laughed, a kind of tired laugh. He must have been driving all night.

I refused to feel anything about that.

I refused, in fact, to feel anything about anything. Dr. John was so good at facilitating that kind of thing. It was hard to manufacture that drifty careless feeling on my own. But I pulled my legs up under me and crossed my arms over my chest and gave it my best shot.

"Right." He sighed and picked up a Styrofoam cup from the middle console, but it was empty and he swore, tossing the cup into the passenger seat footwell. I imagined him stopping at gas stations with me passed out in the backseat of his car, and I was cold to the bone. "Well, that night when the Pastor took you into the—"

"I know which night," I said. I held myself rigid so the memories and their hot, greedy hands would get no hold on me. *Those* memories I'd dealt with. I'd processed the fuck out of them. I'd counseled and therapied. I'd group sessioned and yoga retreated. I'd art therapied and casual sexed them into something I could manage.

I'd cried… I'd cried and I'd cried and I'd cried. And I'd raged and screamed. And then I put them away.

Leaving me with trust issues, insomnia and some stories to tell.

And Jada.

But here they were again, slices like nightmares. The Pastor's hand had smelled like tomato sauce and his breath like soap. The edge of the desk had bit into my thighs. And I thought, I thought with my whole heart that it was over. That I was going to be raped by the Pastor in my Hello Kitty nightgown. But then the door opened and Tommy came in, holding his knife. And he'd screamed. He screamed so loud everything went quiet. I would remember that for the rest of my life.

I didn't get raped, and *that* was my silver lining, for that night was its own kind of nightmare.

Everything after Tommy coming in was hazy.

"They told me he was dead," I said. In the hospital room they'd told me he was dead. That the kids in the house had killed him.

But then my mother showed up. And the nightmare got real.

"I thought all of you were in jail," I said.

"We would have gone to jail," he said. "But this man came in and he made the charges go away. He even took care of the Pastor's wife, who told the police we'd planned to kill both of them and steal from the church."

"Was he a lawyer?"

"No. Opposite of a lawyer, I think. But in return for him doing this, we owed him a debt."

"You fucking killed a guy, and you got to leave for a favor?"

"The man, Bates, he was really powerful. Or worked for a really powerful man at that time. And he pulled the strings to get us out. I can't explain it. I don't know why. It just…happened."

I understood that kind of power. How money could make things go away. How fear could make people do things they normally wouldn't. How some people could walk into a room and make everyone bow to their will—and feel, in the end, like every awful thing they did was right. And just.

My mother had that kind of power. She'd waltzed into that hospital room with her money and her soft, reasonable voice and all her credentials, and it was like she'd never left me. Never hurt me. Wouldn't dream of doing it again.

Yeah, I understood that kind of power.

I lived in fear of that kind of power.

But I didn't feel like being sympathetic.

I was being fucking kidnapped. By my childhood crush. My first love.

Sympathy was squashed out by the heavy fucking irony of it all.

"Sounds ridiculous."

"Yeah," he said quietly. "It really does. But we walked out of that police station, and no one stopped us."

"And none of it explains why you've got me in this car."

"This was the debt."

"Kidnapping me?"

"Picking you up in Santa Barbara and dropping you off in Arizona."

"That makes zero sense, dude."

"I know. But it's happening."

"You know I'm going to have you arrested, right? For kidnapping. I'm going to see you in jail for this shit. The second I get my hands on a phone, you're done."

"That seems about right," he said like going to jail for this was what he deserved, and I sniffed and looked out the window. The sky was getting lighter. My heart was turning to glass.

"People are going to be worried about me," I told him, though frankly it was kind of hard to come up with a list of people who would give a shit.

The US tour was over, and after the debacle in Los Angeles, the European venues were pulling away. Two of them had been canceled altogether. Half my crew had left for Lorde's tour.

I'd fucked up.

My mother said I self-sabotaged.

She was probably right, but I didn't go around admitting it.

"My manager," I said. "Sherman. He'll call the cops. He probably already has."

In front, Tommy nodded.

"Beth. For sure she's freaking out," I said, and he glanced at me in the rearview mirror.

"Your assistant?" he asked.

"Yeah. She does not fool around, and she will be out for your blood—"

"You fired her."

"What?"

"You fired her. Last night before I picked you up."

"You didn't 'pick me up,'" I grumbled, but I frowned. Was that the low-level anxiety I felt about Beth? Had I really fired her? I swallowed my groan and put a hand over my face so Tommy couldn't see my expression in the rearview mirror.

"She stayed though," he said. "After you fired her. She stayed and she tried to protect you from that doctor." He smeared a bunch of disdain all over the word *doctor*, and he wasn't wrong.

I sniffed and watched the rolling red earth outside.

"Where in Arizona are you dropping me?"

"Outside Flagstaff."

Flagstaff. Jesus.

"You better hope it's a spa, Tommy."

"Let's hope it's a spa, then." I glanced up to see a quick smile flash across his face. There and gone. This wasn't funny. None of it was funny.

But his smile was nice. His smile had always been nice. It was the dimple.

And its rarity. How, in those three months, I'd felt special when he turned that smile on me.

Think of something else. Anything else.

But since I was only twenty percent myself these days, and the things I usually thought about—the things that usually crowded my brain, like art and music—weren't there to occupy me...

I couldn't stop fixating on what was happening in my body: the anxious, antsy feeling in my veins, the way my skin didn't fit right and every thought wanted to go someplace dark. This would be about the time I'd make my assistant get Dr. John.

So he could make these feelings go away.

"You have my purse?" I asked. I had a bottle of Ativan in my bag. And an Ativan would really help take the edge off this kidnapping.

"No," he said.

"No phone. No purse. No shoes. I'm giving this kidnapping a shitty review."

I was being ridiculous. I felt ridiculous. I felt like I

was coming apart.

The dog came up over the console to jump into the backseat. She crowded me into the middle, stepping on my hand and flopping over my legs. I suddenly had a lapful of dog.

"Pest," Tommy said, but the dog—Pest, I guess—didn't listen. She licked my hand instead.

"Are you sure this is a dog?" I asked.

"Simon and I thought she was a cat."

I blinked at the casual mention of Simon, and I bit back a thousand questions I had and instead, feeling small and awful, muttered, "Get off me," and shoved the dog away. She whimpered as if wounded by my rejection, and she climbed and flopped back into the front seat.

Comfort had no appeal for me.

The silence was thick and awful, and I wanted to snarl at him. I wanted to sharpen my claws and draw blood. The anxious feeling was growing worse, and it had nothing to do with Beth or not having my phone or even wondering where the hell he was going to take me.

The feeling that my body didn't fit me anymore—it came from the pills and the needles. Or rather it came from not having them.

"Beth?" he said.

"The name's Jada." *Beth doesn't live here anymore.*

"Jada. You all right?"

I wiped a hand over my face, and it came away sweaty. I was beginning to sweat through my shirt. But I was cold.

"Just fine," I said, giving him nothing. Not even my pain.

11

Jada

THERE'D BEEN A time, those heady art-room days, my hands learning the shape of his body through his clothes, that I'd thought I'd recognize Tommy MacNeill anywhere. In the dark, even, by smell.

I would know him by the sound of his breath shuddering in his lungs at the touch of my hand against the bare skin of his waist the few times I'd been brave enough to slip my fingers under his shirt.

There'd been a time I'd thought it impossible *not* to recognize him. Every sense knew him. My body. My heart.

But I saw nothing of the Tommy I'd known, with his shy smile and bright eyes, in this giant man in the front seat.

And if you'd asked me seven years ago if I thought Tommy was capable of something like this, I would have laughed in your face. The kid with the graham crackers was *not* the adult in this car.

"What have you been doing since St. Jokes?" I asked, trying to make my chattering teeth stop chattering. We were climbing a hill, and my ears popped painfully. Everything hurt. This had to be the first stages of withdrawal. Which meant there were going to be more glorious stages. "I mean, is this your first kidnapping, or do you have a little business going?"

He glanced at me, real fast in the rearview mirror, and then back at the road.

And he didn't say a word.

"It's not a hard question," I said. "Unless... if you tell me, you'd have to kill me?" I gasped. "Are you a government agent, Tommy?"

He shook his head.

"Is that a yes?"

"No."

Again more silence.

"Really? The silent treatment? We're not sixteen anymore, Tommy."

"What's talking going to do?" he asked.

I blinked, surprised. At St. Joke's we used to talk all the time. Once I started talking, anyway. But maybe I remembered it wrong. Maybe...maybe all those feelings had just been on my side. Maybe I'd changed things over the years, recast what happened to give me some comfort.

Whatever.

"Keep you awake," I finally said. "Distract me."

"I'm awake."

"Jeez, you turned into an asshole."

I saw his jaw clench, the muscle bulging in his neck. "There's no point, Jada," he said. "I'm dropping you off and driving away."

"Fuck you," I snapped, because the anger felt good and he was being a dick. "Are you honestly going to pretend like you didn't think of me?'

His silence was a brick wall.

"You didn't imagine what I was doing? Where I'd gone? You're not curious?" I cocked my head, waiting for him to say something. His silence egged me on. Infuriated me. "I thought of you all the time. I thought of the art room—"

"Stop."

"You didn't?"

He shook his head, once, a hard shake, like he was trying to dislodge me.

My body lost interest in the withdrawal, the surge of lust in my system distracting it from its cravings for a drug to take the edge off. And oh, did my body find relief in the distraction. I shifted against the seat until my back was against the passenger-side door. At my movement he looked at me over his shoulder, and I was ready for him. My lips parted, my eyebrow cocked.

My shirt slipped over my shoulder, and it didn't go unnoticed by him. Not. At. All.

"I remember the time you put your hand up my skirt—"

"Jada—"

"Remember? You pushed me up against the wall and you held my hand down on the counter—"

"Stop."

"Was that the same time or two different times?" I knew, of course I knew; it was two separate and amazing times. I was just trying to get under his skin. "I can't remember. I've made up so many fucking fantasies about that art room. I've come thinking about—"

"Stop."

No way. "You held my hand down because I kept reaching for you. Putting my hand under your shirt, and you didn't want me to. You didn't like it. And you slipped your hand up under my skirt, remember? And I was so embarrassed by how wet I was. I thought I was gross. That there was something wrong with me. But you…do you remember?"

I could see the blush on his neck and up his face. Across his cheeks. His ears were so red. He didn't nod or shake his head, but he remembered. Oh, he fucking remembered.

I was picking up from exactly where our bodies left

off when we were teenagers.

"What you said?" I asked, leaning forward. "No?" I all but cooed at his silence.

"You liked it," I said. I could feel my body getting hot again as I pulled apart the memory. I pulled it apart and sucked down the marrow, feeding myself with it. "You said I was beautiful. You said—"

"I know what I said," he snapped.

"That I was juicy. That you wanted to taste me."

"Jada—"

"I came, remember. You made me come. My first orgasm."

I laughed in my throat and took out my ponytail, only to put it back in, over and over again, to give my hands something to do.

So I didn't touch him.

Because this kidnapping had taken a turn.

"Do you think about it?" I asked. "Do you remember? The room smelled like turpentine. And the papers on the bulletin board crinkled against my back and I thought you were the most beautiful—"

"I don't want to talk about this," he said, and he turned the radio up so loud I couldn't talk over it.

He'd tried forgetting me, but it hadn't seemed to work.

So now he had to pretend. Well, I wished him luck with that. I was the master of pretending. The queen of make-believe. I'd created a whole world for us in the last seven years. A dream.

That wish kids like us never got to have.

Part of me almost felt bad for him.

Except, you know, he was kidnapping me.

"CAN YOU CHANGE the station?" I asked when the Sports talk and my own thoughts got to be too much for me.

He flipped it to FM, turning the dial until he found a station that wasn't all static. A pop station out of Las Vegas.

"This okay?" he asked.

"Fine."

I knew it was only a matter of time before one of my songs came on and lo and behold, fifteen minutes later the first few chords of "Making Waves" came through the speakers. I was about to ask him to change it when he made a kind of laughing, huffing noise.

Here we go, I thought.

"That's you!"

"That's me."

"I can't believe… holy shit," he breathed and turned it up just a little more. "This song is every-where."

I nodded.

"I can't believe I didn't realize it was you. Your voice. I mean…that's your voice."

I could feel him looking at me in the rearview mirror and suddenly the radio was turned down. "You must be sick of it," he said, all that huffy amazement gone.

His understanding was surprising, the song turned down a relief. "I am. A little."

"How did this happen?"

"I thought you didn't want to talk," I shot back and his silence gave me room to decide whether I wanted to talk or not. He wouldn't—oh, no, not Tommy. No answers from that guy. But I could jabber away. It was so familiar it was almost gross. But I wasn't Beth. If he wasn't going to talk, neither was I.

But then, a few minutes later I was blurting: "I don't know, really. I don't know how it happened."

"No?" he said, without scoffing. With in fact a tremendous amount of the old Tommy empathy. I'd been a sucker for the old Tommy empathy.

"A year ago I got a job on the makeup team for Katy Perry. I was…well, I guess I still am, a body painter and makeup artist. I went on tour with her and did some music videos, and it was a really amazing job for me. I got to do art and be a part of the music world, and it paid really well and it was awesome."

"It sounds awesome."

"At night, I'd do makeup on myself, really wild stuff, and I'd sing cover songs and I'd film it on my computer and upload it onto YouTube. I'd been doing it forever. I'd dress up like a Phoenix and sing an Arcade Fire song. Or a Zombie-nun and I'd sing 'Like A Virgin.' Silly stuff. I got a little following. Nothing huge. Mostly fun. But then I did this mermaid makeup, and I decided to sing an original song. I uploaded 'Making Waves' at like midnight on a Friday night, and I woke up in the morning and it had like seven million views. Two days later I sang on *Ellen* in the full makeup, and a day after that Sherman, my manager, called me to talk about representation, and...well, the rest is history I guess."

"How long ago was this?"

"I uploaded that video seven months ago."

"Holy shit," he breathed. "That's crazy."

"Try living it," I said with a weary laugh. "I don't want to sound like I'm complaining." Because there was nothing worse than someone living a dream life and complaining about it.

"Do you like it?" he asked.

"What's not to like? I get all the finest kidnappings."

"But are you happy?"

"You know, turn up the radio, I don't want to talk anymore."

BY THE TIME we skirted Flagstaff, caught in the traffic of a city waking up and going to work, I was really sick. I couldn't pretend anymore. I was sweating and shaking, my eyes closed in a wince against the daylight. He didn't say anything, didn't bother asking me if I was all right anymore—because it was pretty obvious I wasn't.

He just turned on the heat, blasting the vents into the backseat, but it did little good.

"We're almost there," he said like that was supposed to make me feel better. Give me hope. The other end of this trip promised me nothing.

"Now…you want to talk." I opened my eyes and turned my face to look at him in the rearview mirror, this strange reflective place where our eyes met and then looked away. The distance and the angles made it all feel… safer.

"Who are you dropping me off with?" I asked.

He shook his head. "I don't know."

"What if…what if you're dropping me off to people who are really going to kidnap me?" I swallowed. "Like hold me ransom and shit."

"I'm not going to hurt you," he said.

My laughter had claws that raked at my bones.

"Handing me over to someone who will hurt me…that's hurting me, Tommy. Hate to break it to you."

"No one is going to hurt you."

"You don't know that, do you?" I asked. "Like no one even said that to you. You're just hoping it's true."

I watched his hands squeeze the steering wheel, and I tried not to let it hurt. That I meant so little to him that promising not to give me to someone who would hurt me was a hard thing.

"I won't hand you over to anyone who will hurt you."

"Promise," I said, sharp and fast. Because I was sick. And I was vulnerable. And somehow it was him, here. Tommy. Who'd protected me at my weakest. Who'd charged into that office—a skinny, underfed boy. "Promise me you won't let anyone hurt me. Promise me like you're still the boy who gave me those graham crackers. Promise me like that."

"I promise," he said, but he didn't look at me.

12

Tommy

THE WAY SHE smiled at me when she realized who I was…it was the same way she'd smiled at me when she looked up and saw me walking into the computer lab that day a million years ago.

Like the sight of me made her so happy.

It kicked me in the fucking gut, that smile. Just like it had then.

I still couldn't breathe right.

And all that shit she was talking about those lunch hours in the art room.

She'd thought about it. She'd made herself *come* thinking about it.

I mean…what was I supposed to do with that knowledge? How was I supposed to sit up here and drive and not lose my shit?

And how could she think for one minute that I didn't like her touch on my skin? That I had been in any way repulsed by her?

She'd been beauty personified.

Her hand under my shirt when we were in the art room... If I concentrated, I could pull it up so clearly. Like it was real. Like it was happening now. I'd liked it so much I'd almost come in my pants. I'd been so hard, it had taken every bit of my strength not to lean up against her. Not to grind into her.

God. The things I'd thought... the things I'd wanted.

Still wanted.

Fuck.

It took everything I had not to pull the car over onto the side of the road and just...stare at her. Just take her in. Catalog the changes.

She was beautiful. She was more beautiful than I could have ever imagined. All that beauty combined with something so wild. So artistic and unique.

Beth had turned into something I lacked the imagination to even describe. That inky hair with all its colors, and her eyes so bright and cutting. And she was a woman now, with a woman's body. All that promise realized.

She was tourmaline and I was fucking concrete. But she always had been. And I'd always known it.

My shoulder still burned where she'd bitten me. I reached back to touch it, in the guise of rubbing a sore muscle. But I could still feel the imprint of her teeth.

The small divots. My shirt was damp from her mouth.

Part of me, exhausted and perverse, wished she'd made me bleed.

Blood pounded in my dick and I hated it. Hated myself.

My shoulder would burn for days. Just as my body had burned for years after St. Joke's. The dreams I'd had about her were matches under a fire that never went out.

The clock said 7:50 and I pushed the gas pedal to the floor, sweat crawling down my spine. I had the heat blasting into the backseat, trying to warm up the woman shivering there. I'd never felt so keenly my lack of a jacket. I had nothing to put over her except Pest, and she'd soundly rejected that body heat.

The high-performance engine responded in a na-nosecond, and we hurtled around a semi and a slow-moving pickup truck.

Beth—*no, Jada*—was going into withdrawal. How bad the withdrawal was was going to depend on what she'd been taking and for how long.

I pushed the gas to the floor.

Because I needed her out of this car. And out of my life.

Because she was bringing back all the memories. The fucking *feelings*.

Of us. All of us. Carissa and Rosa and Simon.

Memories of me. The kid I'd been. Starving and so fucking sure I could take care of everyone.

The fucking wishes I'd wished for us. All of them dust now. Mud and shit and nothing.

"Jeez, Tommy, is this some kind of kidnapping race?"

I understood what she was doing. Being a smart-ass because I was scaring her, because she was freaking out.

We all needed armor in this world, and I was glad to see she had hers.

Jada was excellent armor.

It's none of your business, I told myself. *Who she is or what she's become. It has nothing to do with you. You're going to drop her and walk away.*

And not look back.

That was fucking key. I wasn't going to spend the next seven years building a life for her in my imagination. I wasn't going to make small talk and get to know her. I wasn't going to exchange numbers with her and text her in a few days. I wasn't going to imagine her underneath those clothes. The changes the years had made.

I would drop her off, and I would forget her.

I would.

Promise me you won't let anyone hurt me. Promise

me like you're still the boy who gave me those graham crackers. Promise me like that.

I had no reason to believe whoever was on the other end of this drop-off would be there to hurt her.

But there was no reason to believe they wouldn't, either.

There were ten minutes left on the clock, and according to my phone we were still twenty-five miles away.

I took the exit off the highway and followed smaller roads up into the foothills of the San Francisco Peaks.

"I think I'm dying," she said. The first words she'd spoken in a while.

"It's the drugs."

"I know it's the drugs," she snapped. "I just feel like they're making me die."

"Do you know what you were taking?" I asked her.

"Downers after shows so I could sleep. Uppers so I could wake up and perform. There were other prescription things too. The injection was a serious sleeping...thing."

"Sleeping?" I said before I could stop myself. Concern flaring up before I could stop it. She'd always had so much trouble sleeping.

"Yeah, it's still a problem."

I didn't want to know. I didn't want to give a shit.

The things she'd been taking were a cocktail designed for addiction. She was going to have a rough day or two ahead of her for sure. And more in the future. I still had bad days, moments when I'd give anything for some sweet oblivion. And I'd been clean for five years.

"It wasn't...I haven't been doing these drugs all along. It was only...the last part of the tour. Everything was just so intense."

I made a low rumbling noise of understanding.

"I thought I could control it."

I understood that feeling, too, but there was nothing to say, so I kept my mouth shut.

My phone squawked a few more directions at me, and soon I was driving down a long asphalt road, with mesquite growing high and thick on either side. The driveway opened up into a circle in front of an old beautiful adobe mansion with black metal balconies and white curtains fluttering through open windows. The property was groomed with trails and other outbuildings. Flowers bloomed everywhere.

There was even a fountain in front, water spitting from a fish's mouth.

Everything about it said class.

And safe.

I exhaled a breath I'd been holding for what felt like forever and pulled to a stop in front of a discreet sign that read:

Willow Addiction Rehabilitation Facility.

Oh God. Oh thank God.

Giddy with relief, I put my forehead down on my steering wheel.

Rehab. I was driving her to rehab.

The relief was fucking thrilling. All the tension in my body just drained away. For a second I couldn't feel my face.

I put the car in park and turned, not sure how this particular conversation was going to go.

"We here?" she asked. Her eyes were closed and she was shaking, holding on to her thin body with both hands like she might rattle away if she didn't.

"Yeah," I said.

"How bad is it?"

"Open your eyes. It's not bad at all."

"Is it a spa?"

"Not quite." Her eyes blinked open. So brown, her eyes. I'd forgotten how they changed, light and dark depending on the light around her. I saw them now, bloodshot and swimming in tears, and I saw them seven years ago as she sang in that church beside me. I would see them forever, I supposed.

"Rehab?" she said when she saw the sign, and laughed. "This guy you owed a favor to thinks I need rehab?"

"I guess so," I said lamely, because I'd been up for a

solid twenty-four hours at this point and the world was getting fuzzy. And nothing Bates had ever done had made sense.

"I don't need fucking rehab," she said. "It was just a rough month."

I said nothing. I didn't have to.

"Don't do that," she sneered. "Don't judge me."

"I'm not."

I wasn't. I'd been where she was right now, too many times. The judgment she felt was her own.

"You don't want to check yourself in, fine," I said. "Go in and call your people. Call the cops. Go back to your life. I'm just…" *So many fucking things. Too many to name.* "Supposed to drop you here."

"That's exactly what I'm going to do. Call my people. All of them."

But what she needed was this place. And I was pretty sure she knew it.

"Can you walk?" I asked.

"You're a jerk."

"Can you dial a phone?"

"An asshole."

"Can you remember the name of one person who could help you?"

"You could help me and drive me away from here," she said.

I shook my head.

I'd fulfilled my promise, and I had the rest of my life to live, without the shadow of Bates and Beth and St. Joke's over my head. I was going to drop her off, drive to Los Angeles and drown every memory of her in a bottle of whiskey. That's what I was going to do.

I was going to exorcize the ghost of Beth once and for all, or I'd fucking die trying.

And then I was going to get on with my life.

Whatever that meant.

"Maybe," she whispered, wiping her face with a shaking hand. "Maybe I'll stay here a few days, just to get this shit out of my system."

That was good. Excellent. Exactly the right call.

"You want my phone?" I asked. "So you can call the cops?"

It was only fair, after all. I did kidnap her.

She shook her head. "No cops."

I couldn't lie; that was a relief, too.

"Let's get you inside," I said. "We can—"

Beside me Pest barked at something out the windshield, and I turned to see a black woman with her hair in braids had come to stand on the small landing of the main building. She wore a deep purple business suit, and an expression I could only call smug. And I knew smug. Simon was smug as fuck. And this woman… God, it was kind of gross, her standing there in front of rehab looking like she'd been right about every person who walked in those doors.

"Oh my God," Beth whispered, her voice laced with panic and disbelief. Her face when I looked back at her was—if it was possible—even more pale.

And the terror in her eyes…I'd seen that before. And it broke me, that fear. Broke me right in half. Every muscle went on high alert again.

She lurched forward, grabbing the edge of my seat and my hand on the console. Her eyes were sharp and clear and stabbed right through me.

"You can't leave me here," she said.

"Jada—"

"No. Listen to me. I'll go to fucking rehab. Just not this rehab."

"Why?" I asked. She glanced over my shoulder, her lip quivering and her eyes filling with tears. And twenty years from this moment I would still claim, despite everything that happened next, that she wasn't playing me.

She wasn't playing me. Her fear was real.

"I can't go in there with her," she whispered, her voice thick with tears.

"Who is she?" I asked.

"My mother."

13

Tommy

I EXHALED HARD, my body absolutely empty of air. Of anything. I barely had thought left.

"But…" *The fucking debt. If I don't leave her here…*

"Tommy," she whispered. "You said you wouldn't leave me with someone who would hurt me."

"And your mother would hurt you?" I asked.

"That's all my mother has ever done."

Pest barked. Jada's mother had left the front step and was walking toward the car, her face set in careful lines, like she knew what we were talking about.

"Please, Tommy. I'm begging you. Don't leave me here with her."

Her eyes. Oh…God. Her fucking eyes.

Those eyes weren't Jada. They were Beth.

She didn't need to beg.

But I didn't tell her that.

Without saying anything, I started the car and peeled the fuck out of there, my back wheels kicking up gravel at that fountain. In my rearview mirror I saw Beth's mom standing in the driveway surrounded in our dust, watching us go.

Probably getting my license plate tags.

"Thank you," Beth said, sitting back against the seat as if that had taken all her strength. And it probably had.

"Don't thank me yet," I said. "We're going to have your mother, the cops, and Bates after us."

When Bates caught up to me, it was going to be jail or worse.

And I was so tired I couldn't even be upset about it. Some part of me figured the moment I'd picked up that envelope, it was over for me. I'd been living my life in suspended animation since that night, waiting for this.

"Give me your phone," she said, her thin hand reaching forward from the back.

"What are you going to do?"

"Try to get the police off our back, at least."

Good idea or bad, I had no idea, but I handed the phone to her.

"Hey," she said after a few seconds. I glanced in the rearview to see her eyes closed, her hands white-knuckled around my phone. "It's me. I'm borrowing a friend's phone. No. I'm fine. Well… not fine but okay. Yeah, I can imagine. I'm sorry. I am. I know this is a problem. But…I need your help. I'm sorry. But… can you put out a statement. Just tell people I called an old friend to help me get into rehab. I'm looking into a couple of different places and trying to find the best fit."

Man, she had to feel like shit, but she was holding it together like a boss while that asshole made her grovel.

"Yes," she said, "it's true. I'm not exhausted. I'm on too many fucking drugs. I need some time to clean up. Get myself back to normal." She sighed. "I don't know, Sherman. I don't. A week. I know we'll lose more dates in Europe. I know. But…I'll come back so strong I'll be a different person. Yeah," she said. "I'm sure you heard that before. But I'm serious. Thanks. I'll be in touch."

The phone appeared at my shoulder, and I grabbed it, dropping it into the empty cupholder in the middle console.

I should call Simon, I thought. Tell him things had gone south and that he could have my furniture. And I'd finally tell him thank you for taking me to the hospital that night.

I'd tell him when Bates came calling, don't fuck around—just do the job.

"Coming through," Beth said as she crawled up into the front seat, her body bumping against mine as she climbed over the console. Pest whimpered, but she made room as Beth collapsed beside her, directing all the vents onto her shaking body.

"Beth—"

"I'm not Beth," she said. "I'm fucking Jada. And we're going to have to stop somewhere fast; I'm going to get super sick."

Three minutes later I was pulled over on the side of the road while she threw up out the passenger-seat door.

"Can I do anything?" I asked.

"Leave me alone for a few minutes," she snapped, and I grabbed my phone and got out of the car. I whistled for Pest, and she jumped out the driver's side door to find a cactus to pee on.

I didn't have to worry about Jada running anywhere. She was too weak. Too sick and didn't have any shoes. And I wasn't entirely sure if this was still a kidnapping or not.

I turned my back to the sun and called the number Carissa gave me. I expected to leave a message with the robot voice, but Carissa answered on the second ring.

"You're late."

"Yeah." I rubbed at the back of my neck. My shoulder where Jada had bit me still ached like a fucker. "I guess I am."

"So?"

"So there's been a problem."

"No. No, Tommy, there hasn't been a problem. There are no problems. There is only you getting Beth to rehab."

"Her mother was there."

"Right. That was the point."

"She begged me not to leave her with her mother. What was I supposed to do?"

"Are you really still this naive?"

"I'm not fucking naive, Carissa. I grew up in the same places you did."

"And you still believe the addict?"

"Yeah," I said, knowing how that sounded. But I didn't really think she was an addict. "I believe her. She wants help but not from her mother. If you'd seen her face, Carissa…"

"Oh Tommy. You always were a sucker for the new ones." I blew out a long breath. "Tommy, this better not be about sex."

"What?"

"If you're fucking with her—"

"Fucking with her?" My outrage rang false and I knew it. "She's coming off who knows what kind of shit."

"I remember you two when we were kids, you know. Your romance…it felt epic."

"Carissa—"

"It felt like a fairy tale." It had. It totally had. "But this isn't a goddamn fairy tale, and if you are fucking her, I swear to God, Tommy, you won't have to worry about Bates because I will kill you myself."

"I'm not...I won't touch her. But I'm not leaving her with her mother."

"Well, you are in bit of a pickle, aren't you, Tommy?" It was almost funny. If it wasn't my life on the line.

"How much trouble am I in with Bates?"

"That's between you and Bates, but if you want my professional opinion, don't come back to San Francisco, and ditch that car."

And then the line went dead.

I slipped the phone into my pocket and ran my hand over my face and into my hair. My whole body was heavy with weariness. It took so much effort to get myself back to the car, where Beth lay in the passenger seat. Sweating and wretched.

I remembered the feeling all too well.

The urge to take care of her was a tide I couldn't fight.

"Here's the plan," I said, reaching over her to shut the door.

"I'm not going to a hospital," she said. "She'll find me in a hospital. And I know you're not going to believe this, but I'm not that bad. I swear—"

"It's okay. No hospitals," I said in my calmest voice, trying to stop her freak-out. My plan had included a hospital, but there were other plans. "You want to tell me about your mom?"

"No." She laughed. "No. I don't walk to talk about my mom. Tell me about this plan."

"I'm going to check us into a hotel. Drop you there. Get rid of the car and then come back."

"You don't have to," she said. "Come back, I mean. How do we end this kidnapping? I release you from this kidnapping? Do I need to sign something that says I no longer want to be kidnapped by you?"

I'd forgotten how funny Beth could be.

Silly even.

I'd felt, all those years ago, as if I was a post and she was some beautiful bougainvillea—not the purple one but the orange one, the one you rarely saw. I gave her a place to grow, and she made me beautiful.

I shook my head. Fuck. I was tired.

And I wasn't leaving her alone in some hotel room.

"You're going to be sick," I said.

She rolled her head to give me the deadest dead eye. "I hadn't noticed," she said, and I refused to smile. "But you don't have to babysit me."

"It's not just for you," I said. "I haven't slept in a day and a half, and I need to lie low for a while, too."

"The guy...who got you free?"

"Yeah. He's not happy with me."

"I'm not going to apologize."

"You don't have to. It was my job. I fucked it up."

"So, hotel. Lay low. Get better and then…?"

"You go back to your life and I go back to mine."

She sighed and closed her eyes again. "Deal. But if I puke on you, it's your own fault."

An hour later I found a motel off one of the secondary highways. If her mother or Bates were looking for me, it would take some work to find us at the Yucca Family Lodge—swimming pool closed for the season. They offered rooms in the main lodge or cabins you could rent behind the motel. I opted for the cabin at the far edge of the property, checked us in under fake names, said we were there for our honeymoon in the hopes people would leave us alone, paid in cash and got directions for the grocery store in town.

The cabin was about a million times better than I expected. Big vaulted ceilings and hardwood floors. The bathroom was modern, with a tub and shower, and there was even a fireplace on the wall opposite the big queen-size bed. There was a comfortable chair sitting next to the fireplace. An ottoman in front of it. A small table with a lamp beside it.

No television. No neighbors.

Just us.

This would work.

Pest picked her spot on the rug in front of the cold fireplace. I turned up the heat best I could and then went back to get Jada, who was sleeping restlessly in the passenger seat.

"Hey," I said, unclipping her seat belt. "Jada?"

"Yeah?"

"We're here."

"Where?" She fought to open her eyes but kept losing the battle.

"Yucca Family Lodge."

"Sounds…terrible."

"Can I… I can carry you," I offered, but I sounded reluctant to my own ears, like I didn't want to touch her. I'd pushed her away to protect myself. To keep myself sane in this insane situation.

But the situation kept changing.

"No." Her eyes flew open and met mine for just a moment. And I saw her think about how she was going to protect herself. And I was embarrassed that I'd pushed her away. Embarrassed maybe that what I used to feel for her was still so alive. And I still didn't know what to do with it.

I'd never known what exactly to do with Beth.

"I'll walk," she said.

"The ground is rough."

"So am I," she said and pulled herself out of the car. She walked barefoot over the gravel and pine needles rather than be helped by me. Touched by me.

"Wow," she said, standing in the doorway of the cabin, looking at our room. "It's nice."

"I was surprised too."

I got around her into the room and pulled back the thick quilt on the bed. The white sheets and thick pillows looked so tempting, every time I blinked I felt like I was falling asleep.

"You must be tired," she said. She reached for me as if to stroke my shoulder, and then stopped.

I wasn't sure what would happen if she touched me. All the very careful control I was exerting would crumble to dust.

In that moment, with both of us standing there like we'd been carved out of granite, I realized how badly I wanted to touch her.

I was dying to touch her again.

I wanted to roll onto that bed with her and hold her.

Like I was sixteen again. Like I'd never stopped being sixteen.

And being touched by her again? I wasn't sure I could stand it.

"I'm fine," I lied, jerking myself into motion. Forcing the memories away. Pushing the desire down as deep as I could. "I'm going to run into town, hit a grocery store, and see what I can do about the car. Do you have any requests?"

"A new head. A new stomach. Some gum. Skittles."

I smiled. "I'll see what I can find."

She got into bed, sighing with a kind of ecstasy that my exhausted body was deeply jealous of. She caught me staring, and I felt my face get hot, because my thoughts were so far out of my control.

"Oh, Tommy," she sighed. "You have the worst poker face. You always did. When I feel better, we'll give it a shot."

She was talking about sex. About us having sex like it wasn't a big deal. When for me it was too big a deal. Way too big. I turned to walk away, but she grabbed me.

Her hand in mine. Her fingers curled around my thumb. My walls shook.

"I'm...ah...I'm a little scared," she said, her smile bravely losing its battle, and it was over for me. Done. I felt like my heart was in my hand where we touched. I was ice everywhere else, but there, where her fingers clung to mine...

Warm.

I touched her, against all my better judgment. I pushed the hair away from her face so I could see into her amber eyes. Red-rimmed and bloodshot, they filled with tears.

"It's going to be okay," I told her with so little proof.

"Where have I heard that before?" she asked, her lips curved in a smile or a grimace, I couldn't be sure.

But I flinched anyway because the reminder of how I'd failed her put my walls right back up.

"I'm sorry," she whispered.

"For what?"

"For all of this. For making you stay here. For maybe...I don't know...getting you in trouble with Bates or whatever. I'm sorry for the graham crackers."

"You weren't going to apologize, remember?"

"Tommy—"

"Don't!" I snapped. I felt like I was circling a drain, and I didn't have a whole lot of strength left. "This isn't your fault. None of it is."

I was exhausted. I was stressed and scared. I was worried.

And it was Beth here.

My Beth.

Seven years later and I was locked in this cottage with her with nowhere to run. Nowhere to go.

It was her and me, and I'd dreamed about a version of this more times than I could count.

She's going to get fucking sick, you degenerate pig.

Right. And that.

"This is my fault. I got you into this mess, Jada," I said. "You feel like shit because of the drugs, but you're going to wake up in two days and see that this is pretty much my fault."

"Oh, that's right. You kidnapped me." She smiled a

little as she said it.

"I did. I kidnapped you."

Her breath shuddered and she closed her eyes and I expected to see her cry. I expected tears to stream out from under those outrageous lashes. I expected to watch the tears bathe those freckles I so dearly loved.

"I can't pretend," she whispered.

"Pretend what?"

"That I'm not me." Her eyes opened, those amber eyes so familiar I knew them in my bones. "That you're not you."

I blinked and nearly said, very nearly said, *I will. I will pretend for both of us.*

But I kidnapped her and she felt like shit, and it was only going to get worse.

"You don't have to," I said and she sighed. She sighed with such relief. Like my words gave her comfort. I regretted them in a heartbeat, and at the same time I regretted that I hadn't said them earlier. The minute I saw her on that bed in Santa Barbara, I should have told her.

It's me, Tommy, and I loved you once. I won't hurt you. I will protect you.

I was ashamed that my instinct had been to turn away from her.

My fingers reached for her face, the blue curl over her ear. I nearly brushed it back but stopped myself just in time.

No touching. I couldn't do this and not pretend. I couldn't do this, not pretend *and* touch her.

"Go to sleep. I'll be back."

She smiled as her eyes fluttered shut. "So bossy. All the time."

Everything I wanted not to feel, it was here. In the air around us, and she sighed. We were connected. We always had been. Pretending didn't change anything.

"I'm leaving Pest here," I told her. "Don't open that door for anyone. I'm serious. I'll be back in an hour." I dragged a garbage can nestled in the corner by the dresser, over to her bed in case she was sick. Which was inevitable. "Get some sleep if you can."

"Thank you, Tommy."

"It's okay…Beth."

And that was the end of pretending.

TOWN WAS A long fifteen minutes away and I picked up some necessities at the tiny mom-and-pop grocery store. Gatorade and bottled water. Applesauce and chocolate pudding that didn't need to be refrigerated. Some loaves of bread and peanut butter and jelly. A bunch of oranges. Kibble for Pest.

I looked at it all on the conveyor belt as I waited to pay and realized it was exactly what Simon and I lived on those first few months in that apartment. It was the diet he'd prescribed because it had protein and vitamin C. We'd been broke and scared, and I was growing so big so fast that at night my bones hurt. And there had never been enough food. Not ever.

But there'd been more with Simon than at St. Joke's. He made sure of it.

And now… I was back at the same survival menu.

My life was traveling in large loops. Constant circles. With minor variations.

Not Simon this time but Beth. Not Beth…Jada.

Fuck. I was tired.

The magazines on the rack beside the checkout were full of Jada. Pictures of her in the mermaid costume, with the long curly wig and the mask, seemed to be the favorite.

And I understood why; it was sexy. That outfit. The whole look was sexy, and not just because she showed a lot of skin above the iridescent tail she wore. The body paint made the most of her thin stomach and the bikini top pushed her breasts together.

It was sexy because it was so outrageous. So bold. Confident.

Fucking ballsy. So ballsy I had to smile. I wanted to laugh.

Because she didn't care what other people thought of her. She'd committed to this idea that no one would know who she was. That's what the costumes were. The masks and the wigs. It was her protecting herself, and I understood that in my gut.

Difficult pop star passes out onstage, said one of the headlines.

On another there was a grainy picture taken from a cell phone of Beth wearing a long blonde wig and a unicorn horn, passed out on the stage, her band rushing to her side.

Exhaustion? said the headline. *Or a difficult artist's drug-fueled lifestyle?*

Man, they loved calling women difficult.

I couldn't even imagine what her life had been like the last seven months. How do you cope with that kind of change? That kind of sudden pressure?

I turned the magazine around and put it back on the plastic shelf, the pictures of Jada hidden.

There was no leaving her. Even if she'd given me ten names of people who could drive out here and bring her shoes and her phone and money. The fact that she had no one made me so lonely for her I couldn't stand it.

Maybe because I got it.

I had Simon and that was it. And he really was only in my life because he was gone half the time. Most of the time.

My only friend was never in the country and rarely had cell service.

It's why we stayed friends.

I'd kept all the spaces around me clear. All the spots that would have been occupied by girlfriends or friends or even lovers, I kept them blank.

Because it felt better that way. Safer.

None of that did me any good here.

None of that distance kept me safe because now I was locked up in a cottage with the girl I'd failed and the girl I'd loved and the girl I'd never forgotten.

On the outskirts of Prescott there was a used car dealership, dusty and sun-blasted, its red and white flags hanging limp in the windless day. I took a sharp right into the lot that had plenty of old SUVs and pickup trucks.

The salesman came out to greet me, buttoning his sports coat over his stomach. "Hey there," he said, all smiles. "What can I do you for?"

"Straight-up trade," I said.

"Your BMW?" the man asked, looking dubious. "For what?"

I pointed to a truck exactly like the truck I had at home. "For that."

The salesman wanted to check the blue book and he would have to call the owner to see if he could give me that kind of trade, but I waved him off and a half hour later I was driving back to the Yucca Family Lodge in a stripped-down 2007 gray Ford pickup.

The salesman could figure out how much money I

should have gotten for the BMW, while he also figured out how much it was worth to him to take my advice and park the BMW in the back for a few weeks just to be on the safe side.

"Safe from what?" he'd asked.

"All sorts," I'd said and gotten out of there.

I opened the cottage and found it just as I left it, Jada…Beth in bed, the covers pulled up to her ears and Pest beside the bed.

Pest lifted her head as I came in, and I put our stuff on the dresser and poured Pest a bunch of kibble. I collapsed in the chair that sat next to the fire, and Pest, when she was done with her meal, came to sit beside me.

I reached down and pulled her up into my lap. I'd spent years trying to train the lap squirrel not to be a lap squirrel. But I figured we could both use a little contact.

I stared at the bed and tracked the slow rise and fall of Beth's breathing.

My breathing began to match hers, and I thought, sleep creeping over me: *This is how long it takes. Half a day, a few minutes of quiet and my body lines itself up along hers again.*

I couldn't stop it. Didn't even know how.

"Pest?" I said, and my old friend licked my thumb in response. "What the hell are we going to do now?"

14

Beth

I CRIED MY first night at St. Joke's. I didn't, like, sob. Or howl. I just leaked. Tears streaming out of my eyes. I couldn't talk. Or eat. I didn't want to. I just wanted my mom. As crazy as that seemed, as much as she had put me through, I just wanted her to walk in that door and pull me up from that kitchen table and get me out of there.

But it didn't happen.

Instead the Pastor's wife got pissed and took my dinner away, and the Pastor said anyone giving me food would get punished.

Around that table were four kids who didn't even look at me when he said this. They stared at their plates and nodded. I didn't expect any of them to help me. I'd watched those movies and read the books—I knew what foster homes were like.

When the lights went out, they'd probably take turns beating me up.

"Girls," the Pastor said, leaning back from the table. Tommy, the big blond kid, started shoveling in the rest of the meager amount of food he'd been given. "Clear the table."

Carissa and Rosa jumped to their feet, and I lurched to mine. I had no plates of my own to pick up, so I picked up Simon's. Carissa picked up Tommy's, and he handed her his spoon and looked at me. I was startled by the brush of his blue eyes. By the way his gaze seemed to pierce me. I leaked more tears and all but ran into the kitchen.

It was drab and gray.

All the cupboards had locks on them. So did the refrigerator.

I stared at those locks and felt real terror.

That night as we were all getting ready for bed, the girls in the downstairs bathroom, the boys in the upstairs bathroom, Carissa shouldered into the bathroom next to me and whispered, "Tommy has something for you."

"What?" I asked.

She shrugged.

"How...how do you know?"

"He gave me his spoon at dinner and looked at you."

It didn't make any sense.

I expected something awful. Something dirty.

These kids were so rough—nothing like the kids I went to school with or the kids I had carefully monitored study sessions with. I expected, even while crying, to be hurt.

When I passed Tommy in the hallway, he tried to hand something to me, and I flinched away and a sleeve of crackers in brown waxy paper fell on the floor.

Simon picked them up.

"Are you trying to get in trouble?" Simon asked Tommy in the thinnest, quietest whisper imaginable.

"I'm trying to get her something to eat," Tommy whispered back. Both of them were watching the staircase like a monster was going to come up. Tommy grabbed the crackers from Simon and shoved them at me.

"Take them," he said. He had the bluest eyes. And the whitest hair. "You didn't have dinner."

I stood there, silent and leaking.

"Hey," he said in a softer voice. "It's okay. You're hungry, aren't you?"

I nodded, because I was. I was hungry and scared, and this boy's voice and this package of crackers was a kindness when I hadn't felt any in a long time.

"Thank you," I whispered, and I took them.

"You're welcome," he said and I caught him smiling at me, so I smiled back. And for just a second, a split second, things felt…better. Brighter.

Simon tapped Tommy on the shoulder and jerked his thumb toward the room they shared.

"I'll see you tomorrow," Tommy said, and he and Simon left. I stood there for a second, the crackers in my hands. My eyes dry for the first time in days.

Tommy, I thought.

And then I went into the room I shared with Rosa, the pregnant girl. I didn't like this room. It was ugly and cold and the window didn't open and the sheets were scratchy and smelled like bleach. I missed my double bed and all my pillows. I missed my sheets that smelled like lavender because Mom believed lavender would calm me down before bed. And I missed my books and my guitar and even though she was a monster, I missed my mother so much it hurt.

It hurt to breathe.

"You have to stop crying at some point," Rosa said. She wasn't even looking at me and she knew I was crying.

"I'm trying," I whispered and hiccuped.

"Well, you gotta try harder."

"Do you want a cracker?" I asked her, tearing them open on our desk. According to my old biology textbook, pregnant women had to eat more calories.

"What the hell are you doing?" Rosa asked, grabbing the crackers and handing them to me and then sweeping the crumbs off the desk. She licked the crumbs off her hand.

"You're hungry—"

"Tommy give you those?" she asked, and before I could answer, she shook her head. "Fucking Tommy. You get caught with those, you're in trouble, you get that?"

I didn't. I didn't get anything. The tears started again, and Rosa rolled her eyes. She grabbed the crackers and put them under my pillow. "You get caught with them, you say Tommy gave them to you."

"Will he get in trouble?" I asked. There'd been a whole bunch of rules when I got moved here. All kinds of binders and pamphlets, and I didn't pay attention to any of them. I was numb.

"Better him than you."

"I'm not going to tell on him." I didn't know a lot, but I knew telling on someone wasn't going to win me any friends.

"You do what you want," she said like she was washing her hands of the whole thing.

We got into our pajamas with our backs turned to each other. Shrugging out of our shirts and our bras and throwing our clothes over our bodies like someone might catch us naked. I was curious about her stomach, I'd never seen a pregnant teenager, but I didn't look.

"Good night," I said when we were both in bed, and I reached over to turn off the light on the table between us.

"You have to leave it on until he comes up and turns it off."

"The Pastor?"

She nodded, and something cold slid over me. I didn't like the Pastor, and I rolled over onto my side and pulled a cracker out of the sleeve from under my pillow. I nibbled an edge and thought about Tommy.

Those eyes couldn't be real. No one had eyes that blue.

"Girls?" The Pastor's voice made me jerk, and I shoved the cracker under my pillow before rolling over to face him.

"What's under your pillow?" the Pastor asked, his runny eyes focused on me like lasers, and I said nothing. I froze. I couldn't even swallow the cracker that was in my mouth.

He walked across the room to my bed, his belly shaking with every step. Small tremors and earthquakes. As he got closer, I could smell him, wine and something else. Something I didn't like.

"I asked you a question, Beth."

"Nothing," I said, lying badly because I never lied very well.

Rosa didn't say anything; she was looking at her

hands folded over her stomach. The Pastor reached under my pillow, his other hand grazing my hip, and I flinched away from him. His touch felt poisonous. Like his breath. His smell. Everything about him gave me the creeps.

"Where did you get these?" he asked, holding up the crackers.

I was silent. Terrified. Tears pouring down my cheeks.

"Rosa?" he asked, and she looked up so fast I saw her fear before she put it away.

"I don't know where she got them," she said.

He sat on the edge of my bed, his weight making a dip so I rolled toward him. My whole body pressed against his leg, and my stomach curled. "Beth," he said, putting his hand on my knee. I couldn't breathe with him so close. "You're not in trouble. But stealing food is against the rules."

His hand squeezed my knee and Rosa made a low, scared sound in her throat and I nearly threw up.

"Tommy," I said. So much for trying to make friends. So much for not tattling. So much for me being brave. "Tommy gave them to me."

The Pastor stood, his expression so pleased. So satisfied. Like he'd known all along and being proven right was just the best thing.

I knew that expression because I saw it on my

mother's face all the time.

She loved that I disappointed her.

"Thank you, Beth," he said. "Honesty is always rewarded."

And then he turned off the light and shut the door and I heard the loud *click* of a lock.

"He's locking us in?" I asked Rosa, my voice shaking.

"He always does."

"What...what is going to happen to Tommy?" I asked.

"Nothing he didn't deserve. The boy knows the rules."

That didn't comfort me.

I wasn't crying anymore. Fear and adrenaline and guilt kept my eyes dry and awake.

Awake long enough that hours later I heard the footsteps coming up the stairs. A door was unlocked. Not ours.

I sat up.

There was a rumble of voices. Tommy said something. I couldn't make it out.

And then there were two sets of footsteps walking down the hall toward the room at the end of the hallway. The office, someone called it.

"Go to sleep," Rosa said. "There's nothing you can do."

But I was sick with the truth.

There was nothing I could do because I'd already done it.

I WOKE UP out of my dream, sweaty and foul, my stomach and my head in a war. My body ached so much it felt like I had the flu. I thrashed in sheets that smelled like St. Joke's.

Sour sweat and bitter fear.

"Hey," a soft voice said. "It's okay. You're okay."

I turned toward the comfort of that voice because I had no defenses. My eyes blinked open against their will, but the cabin we were sharing was dark. Only a fire in the fireplace. I sighed because the darkness was appreciated. I was sure I looked like shit. And I didn't want to face the bright light of anything. Not yet.

"You want something to drink?" Tommy asked and I nodded. He'd been taking care of me for I wasn't even sure how long. Hours. Days. Weeks. Most of my life.

"Thank you," I said, gratitude getting brittle on my tongue.

He helped me with a bottle of water, and I fell back against the bed after a sip like I'd run a marathon.

"I feel terrible," I said. "Like the flu and hangover all in one."

"I have some painkillers. Over-the-counter stuff." I

heard the rattle of a bottle, and then he pressed two pills into my hand, his fingers cool against my skin.

I swallowed the pills with more water and fell back against the bed.

"Want some orange?" he asked.

"Orange what?"

"Orange…orange," he said, and I smiled because I could hear in his voice that he was smiling too.

"I was hoping for Skittles."

"I'm sure you were. But orange orange is what I'm offering."

"Orange sounds… amazing."

His low, rumbly laugh filled the room. And then there was a peeled orange segment in my hand, the velvety skin just barely containing the juice and pulp. I put it in my mouth and burst it with my teeth.

I groaned in ecstasy.

"Let's not get carried away," he said, teasing me.

"I remember the way you used to eat peanut butter sandwiches, so don't give me any grief. Oh my God, and bologna. You loved bologna."

It was silent for a moment, like I'd crossed some line, and I turned my head to find him in the shadows.

You said, I wanted to say, *you said I didn't have to pretend.*

For a second it almost seemed like he was scared, but the expression was gone so fast I could have only imagined it. Seeing things in the shadows.

"I felt that way about everything I got to eat."

"He starved you."

"I think actually…she did. But yes, I was hungry. A lot."

"Someone fed you," I said, lifting my hand to wave at his body.

"Simon mostly," he said. "Once we got out, he made sure I got enough to eat."

"Sounds sweet," I said.

"It wasn't at the time, but looking back at it…" He shrugged.

"I'm glad you killed him. The Pastor—"

"Beth—"

"Don't," I whispered, though I wasn't sure what I was saying that about. *Don't pretend like killing him wasn't exactly right. Don't deny this past.*

He handed me another piece of orange, and I put it in my mouth, the juice running down the corner of my lips. I wiped it away with the back of my hand, feeling like the kid I'd been with him.

"Where is everyone?" I asked. "Simon and Carissa and Rosa?"

He was silent for a long time. So long it hurt.

"It's conversation, Tommy. I'm not sucking your dick."

He made some noise in the shadows, a noise that

woke up my blood. That cleared some of the fog. Oh, how I'd dreamed of sucking his dick, and that noise... that noise told me he'd dreamed of it too.

"Simon is a journalist," he finally said.

"That totally makes sense."

He nodded like he agreed.

"Rosa went to jail. She gets out soon."

"No," I gasped. "The baby?"

"With the dad. Simon keeps tabs on them."

That made my heart hurt.

Tommy handed me another orange, and I shook my head.

"You need to eat something," he whispered. "Rosa will...she'll be okay. Simon and me, we put some money aside for her. She'll get out and she'll get to know her kid and she'll be okay."

When would he stop taking care of us, I wondered.

I took the orange. "What about Carissa?"

"I think she works for Bates."

"The guy that got you out of jail?"

He nodded, the skin on half his face glowing from the fire.

"No shit?"

He shrugged. His face didn't change. He didn't shift or flinch. Nothing. But I knew he was bothered by the thought of Carissa working for Bates.

"I missed you," I said, the words spilling out of my

mouth bathed in the scent of an orange he peeled for me with his blunt, rough fingers. "Every day for a long time. Years, even. I missed you."

This was where I should tell him I'd looked for his family. His grandpa, the lemon farmer outside of Santa Barbara. It was the right thing to do, but somehow I couldn't make the words come. I knew when I told him, it would hurt him. And he'd be furious. And I didn't want that.

In his silence I heard a lot of things, and I waited for him to say them out loud. How he missed me. How he thought about me.

Tell me. Say it. One way or another say it so I can stop feeling like this. Like I imagined what we'd meant to each other.

"More orange?" he asked. His eyes met mine in the glow of the fire.

This is all I can give you. That was what he was really saying. *This is all you'll get from me.*

I took the slice, murmuring my thanks.

Like that was enough.

I shivered under the blankets.

"Cold?" he asked.

"I'm fine," I lied.

"I'll build up the fire."

I heard him on the far side of the room. I could

smell the wood burning and it was so fucking comforting.

"Better?" he asked.

I nodded, though I was still shaking. The cold was inside me, and I wasn't sure there was a fire big enough or hot enough to change that.

And it hurt, that he so badly didn't want to know me. Or what had happened to me. When all I wanted, all I wanted on this earth was to know what had happened to him.

"Jada?" he asked.

And then his hand cupped my shoulder, his big palm ran over my arm down to my elbow and then my wrist and back up, the calluses scraping against my freezing flesh.

"I missed you, too," he said.

In an instant I was warm.

15

Beth

I WOKE UP again, bright light piercing my eyelids through a set of curtains. The lingering fingers of a nightmare stroked my face, burrowed into my brain.

"Mom?" I whispered, because she'd been here in my dream. Sitting in a chair waiting for me to wake up. She'd been talking to the doctors, putting me on prescriptions. *I've got to get out of here.*

"Your mom's not here," Tommy said, and it all settled back around me like pieces of a puzzle.

"Well," I said, flopping back onto the bed. "That's good news."

"How are you feeling?" Tommy asked. He'd pulled the chair up to the bed, and he sat close enough he could put his feet up on the end of the mattress. I imagined him watching me while I slept and did not feel bad about it.

"How am I feeling," I said and closed my eyes. "Let me check."

The low rumble of his chuckle went over my body like ripples through a puddle.

I held myself still and did the test. The percentage test. How much of me was…me? It took me a second, my body feeling both tiny and huge at the same time. Like I was a doll that had been pulled apart and then put together again all wrong.

But slowly I made sense of myself. Organized my body in a way I recognized. Or…would recognize, maybe. If given some time.

Sixty percent. I was sixty percent myself. And sixty percent was pretty freaking great.

Ravaged and thin and embarrassed and scared. But me. My thoughts were in my head. I could feel my body—not just in pieces but the whole thing. There was no fog. No anxiety.

"I feel…like me," I said, which didn't make any sense, but he had the grace not to say anything. The blankets fell from my shoulders as I struggled to get up. He reached over and helped me, his big hand and incredible strength lifting me up in the bed like it was nothing.

When he pulled back his hand, I wanted to grab it. I wanted to grab him.

But I remembered with a slight cringe of embarrassment telling him how much I missed him and him, in response, handing me an orange.

"Here." Tommy had a glass of water and a bottle of Gatorade in his hands. His beard had grown in, and he looked good in it. "Water or Gatorade?"

"Both," I sighed. He handed me the water first, but I reached for the Gatorade instead. *Yay, sugar.* "What time is it?"

"It's about eight in the morning," he said.

"I've been asleep for a day?" I asked, unable to put together all my crappy memories. I'd been sick. A lot. He'd tried to help me, but I just about bit his head off for trying. I remember taking pain medication from him every few hours, over-the-counter stuff that did nothing to soothe the beast living inside my veins.

"Pretty much."

"Is it weird that I expected it to be worse?"

"Nothing is weird," he said. "And don't get cocky. Nothing is over. Drugs have a way of sticking with you."

"Are you speaking from experience?" I asked, even though I knew. I knew because I could see it in the corners of his eyes and the way he held his shoulders and looked at me and then away so fast.

He nodded and then shrugged like it was no big deal, and I wanted to curl up in his lap like that damn dog and ask him to tell me more, tell me everything.

But he'd made it clear we weren't going down that road.

So instead I tipped the bottle to my mouth and some of the Gatorade splashed on my neck but I just used my T-shirt to soak it up.

The sweet, orangey drink tasted like heaven. I felt, with every gulp, my body waking up.

"Careful," he said. "Your stomach is still pretty fragile."

I was all wrung out and flush at the same time. I wanted to take off my clothes and stretch out in the sunshine. I imagined, for one delighted, scandalous moment, what he would do if I did that. If I just stood up and stripped.

And then I decided I wasn't tough enough at the moment to handle his inevitable rejection. Not even Jada could do that.

Besides, I needed a shower. For real.

"You want to tell me about your mom?" he asked.

"No," I said. He was killing my happiness.

"You were having a nightmare and you were yell-ing—"

"I thought we weren't talking."

He nodded, though I could tell he wanted to argue.

"Have you slept?" I asked. He looked worn and tired. Fuzzy and red-eyed.

"Not much."

"Have you eaten?"

"Some."

"You should eat that orange and take the bed," I said, scrambling out of the way, caught in the blankets. God, I was wrapped up like a sweaty burrito, I must have had some kind of nightmare.

"You want a shower?" he asked.

I gasped. With delight I gasped, and the rough crackle of his laugh brushed over me. Waking me up.

"I guess yes. Come on." He held out his hand for me, like he was going to help me out of bed. He had to be so tired. He was beside me every time I woke up with a bottle of water or a slice of orange. A warm hand on my shoulder.

"I'm going to change my rating on this kidnapping," I said. "It's pretty five star."

"I appreciate that," he said, that dimple reappearing like an old friend.

I wondered—before I could stop myself, in a purely Beth frame of mind—if he treated everyone like this. Or if I was special.

It hurt how much I wanted to be special.

But that was fucking Beth for you, wasn't it?

I pushed the sheets off my body. My skirt was up around my waist and my shirt hung off my shoulders. I was revealed in pieces. My shoulder blade. My hip. The black satin of my underwear.

Tommy looked away so fast, and the tips of his ears burned red.

My body made him blush.

My body had—for the last few months, since the "Making Waves" video—just been a thing. Part of the show. Like the lights and the sound. It was the thing that wore the costume. The body paint.

It was a tool. Like my voice. And a microphone.

But with Tommy in the room, my body was my body again. Private again.

That shouldn't be exciting. It had no business being exciting.

But it was.

It was exciting that he was looking at me. Like I was a person. A woman.

I stood up on shaky legs and pulled down my skirt. Fixed my shirt. When what I wanted to do was take it all off. Show him something super private.

After the shower, maybe.

After his nap.

I got excited about the idea, answering the question we'd been asking each other in that art room.

What would it be like between us? I remember thinking it would be perfect. That I wouldn't be scared. I'd known enough that he would take care of me.

To a surprising degree, I still wanted that.

"Need help?" he asked, half turned away, the sunlight through the window lighting up the whiskers on his face.

He was beautiful. He always had been. And his body... the wideness of it. The thickness.

It was beautiful too.

In the stillness of my body there was a spark. Like a rusty old BIC lighter that had been found in the mud.

A flicker. Desire. Interest.

How predictable I was. How predictable my reaction. And wasn't that a fucking relief.

There was no stopping the smile that crossed my face.

"Beth?" he asked, and I shook my head, shaking off the thoughts of Tommy's body. Of Tommy's body pressing me into this bed. I imagined, before I could stop it, his hand up under my skirt again, his other hand holding my wrist. I imagined his breath against my face as he whispered, *I want to taste you.*

I'd played a lot of games with other lovers that mirrored that scenario—but it had never come close to the feeling I'd had with Tommy.

How much longer, I wondered, would we be here? And how much effort would it take to get him to stop pretending he wasn't thinking of me the exact same way I was thinking of him?

"Did I throw up on you?" I asked, suddenly horrified by the thought.

"No."

"Are you lying to make me feel better?"

"I wouldn't lie about you throwing up on me. But you called me some incredibly interesting names."

"I didn't mean it."

The dimple in his cheek made a sudden and quick appearance, and in my weakened state I was reduced to being sixteen again, transfixed by this man's smile. Immobilized by his attention.

"You meant a few of them," he said.

I shuffled my way over to the bathroom. The rustic floorboards were smooth and cool beneath my feet.

"I don't have any clothes," I said.

"I picked up a few things. There weren't a whole lot of choices, but I got you the basics."

"That's…nice."

"Well, wait until you see the shirt."

He grinned and I felt warm all over.

That delicious tickle in the back of my mind. The sudden awareness between my legs. The heady thrum in my blood.

"While you shower," he said, "I'll take Pest for a walk, if that's okay? She hasn't had much of a chance, and she's getting a little restless."

"Yeah. Of course. Please. I'll be fine."

He turned the water on for me, testing it to make sure it wasn't too hot, and I held on to the pedestal sink.

The bathroom was small with him in it. Maybe the

world was small with him in it. I'd been around big guys. The last few months had been a never-ending parade of bodyguards and security. Men who wore their muscles like a suit of clothes that didn't always fit great.

Tommy was big in a body he was born in.

Did that make sense? I couldn't tell. But his hands were big. His arms and thighs. He wasn't fat—not in any way, but his waist was big. He was just thick. Solid. He wore a gray T-shirt, and he filled out every inch of it with himself. His jeans too. His boots.

Steam started to spill out of the shower, and my skin was flushed from the heat. Every breath I pulled in tasted like the beginning of something.

His presence was big. It always had been. I wondered if he knew that. If he understood that's why all us kids in that foster home had gravitated toward him. It was because he was a huge light in a terrifying darkness.

"Jada?" He hadn't called me by name, my real name. Not this entire time. It was a little amazing how much I wasn't Beth to him.

Even more amazing was how—at this moment—I wanted to remind him of who I was. Who I'd been.

Who we'd been.

"You know why I liked sitting next to you?" I asked, the words spilling from cracked, dry lips. "When we were kids?"

He shook his head, looking as if I'd stunned the words right out of him.

"Because I felt like no one could see me if I was beside you. Like I was perfectly hidden in the shadow of your body."

"Not hidden enough," he said, but I didn't want to talk about that. About that night and what had happened to all of us.

"I also liked sitting next to you because you were warm. Sitting next to you was like sitting in the sun. It felt so good."

He glanced away, fidgeting with the water. I watched him swallow. "Your clothes are over there," he said, jerking his thumb over his shoulder at the three big baskets in the corner. A small stack of clothes sat on top of one.

I touched his hand, the bone of his wrist, the vein just under his skin. I wanted to put my body next to his and let him warm me up again. I expected him to jerk his hand away, but instead he grabbed on to mine. Holding my fingers carefully in his grip, and just that touch, that little thing turned me on.

"It's not real, what you're feeling," he told me. I didn't play dumb or ask him what he meant; I knew what he meant.

"How do you know?"

He was silent. Right…because he'd come down off his own highs. Recalibrated his own system after weeks of trying to destroy it.

"It feels real." I squeezed his hand. I slipped my fingers between his, the calluses so rough it was like getting scraped by a scrub brush. "It feels familiar."

He shook his head.

"You don't remember how good it felt? You don't want to feel that way again, just…for a little while?"

He left without another word.

"Was it something I said?" I asked the scarecrow in the mirror.

16

Beth

THE SHOWER WAS a revelation. I stayed until the water went cold, and even then I stayed a little bit longer. I felt both completely restored and totally drained coming out of it. I wrapped a towel around my hair and grabbed my new clothes from the baskets.

Good God, where did he find fuzzy socks covered in smiling face emoticons—and did he remember Mr. Abrahams's socks from that day in the art room? They'd been eerily similar.

Did he remember? was becoming a refrain in my head.

Black cotton underwear. A cotton sports bra thing. Black leggings, a little big, but everything was going to be big on me—I needed about twenty cheeseburgers.

And a T-shirt with a wolf howling at the moon on the front of it.

There was a tag that claimed it glowed in the dark.

That's why he'd been smiling. Well, joke's on him. I

loved wolf-howling-at-moon T-shirts. I slipped it over my head, gathered the bottom hem in a knot in the back, and grabbed the plastic comb I'd found on the edge of the sink.

I opened the door of the bathroom into the chill of the bigger main room only to find Tommy passed out on the chair. Pest, covered in leaves and having tracked in dirt, was sleeping again by the fire.

Tommy filled the chair. His hands hung loose by his sides. His head was turned away toward the window like he was giving me privacy and room even in his sleep.

Such deference.

It was weird. Or maybe what was weird was how used to not having privacy I'd gotten.

He'd taken off his boots and one of his socks hung off his toes, and it...it was adorable. Before I realized entirely what I was doing, I'd reached over and pulled it back onto his foot. His toes where they should be. His heel.

His long foot snug in a nondescript white athletic sock. The arch warm in my hand.

The way his hand had been in mine when we were kids. The way his bicep had curved to fit my palm. The back of his neck. The hard length of his cock under the fly of his jeans.

I remembered every single part of his body that I'd

measured with my palm.

On the bed were a stack of clean sheets he must have picked up from the front desk, wherever that was. Were we still in Arizona?

Quickly I pulled the dirty sheets off and replaced them with the clean ones. And then I sat on the corner of the bed, brushing out my long hair. My roots were showing. My nails were ragged. I was a mess.

Tommy was too, I supposed, but all his rough edges only looked good on him.

The blond stubble on his cheeks, the creases around his eyes.

As I watched his chest lifting and falling with every breath, his head bobbed forward and he jerked it back, glancing around with blurry eyes before shutting them again. Beside him Pest whined as if asking me if I was really going to let her master sleep there so uncomfortably.

I got up off the bed and crouched beside his chair.

"Tommy?" I whispered, and his eyes opened at once.

"What's wrong? You okay?"

I smiled, tenderness biting at my throat. "I'm fine. But why don't you go lie down on the bed. You're so tired and I changed the sheets."

"I'm okay," he sighed, his eyes slipping shut.

"No," I said in a louder voice. I stood and grabbed

his hand. It was hot and rough, that hand. So rough. "Wow," I said, running my fingers over the calluses, every edge elevated to something erotic. I felt the texture of his hands on every part of my body he wasn't touching. "You sand wood with these?"

He smiled but pulled his hands away from me, clenching them into fists. "I could, probably."

"I was teasing," I said, feeling like I'd wounded him somehow.

"I know." But still it felt like I'd crossed a line.

"Tommy," I whispered, unsure of what to say, only that something needed to be said. "We used to be—"

His blue eyes met mine, and I think because he was so tired, he let himself look at me. Really look at me. And maybe he'd been doing that all night, but I doubted it. I felt keenly my lack of makeup. I had no more armor. No more Jada and not even lipstick to hide behind.

All my freckles, it felt, were glowing.

To my utter surprise he lifted a finger and touched the freckle at the top of my lip. The calluses, rough on my hand, were electric on my face, the sensitive skin of my lip, and I gasped.

My lips parted and his finger shifted, from my top lip to my bottom, abandoning the freckle to touch, just barely, the damp skin of my lower lip, at the edge of my mouth. My heart stopped. My breath stopped.

Conscious thought stopped.

Tommy.

Was.

Touching.

Me.

My tongue tasted the salt of his finger. My body went wet in one wild cataract of lust. A wave I was swept up in.

"I know what we used to be," he murmured, his voice so low I felt the bass of it in my own chest. "And of course I remember everything we did in the art room." His finger was at the edge of my mouth. Not inside. But not *not* inside. I was torn apart by the exactness of it, how I could feel, even as he touched me, his restraint. "I remember every second of the art room. I've turned those memories over in my mind a thousand times. I dream about the art room, too. So many fucking dreams."

"Tommy," I breathed.

My hair was down, water straightening out the curls into a long damp sheet on my back, making my shirt wet, and he leaned up in the chair, his finger leaving my mouth to touch my hair, to gather it up in his hands. Holding it in his fist.

"I remember how you tasted. How you felt. I re-member holding your hand down on the desk, not because I didn't like you touching me. Never that. But because I liked it so much. I nearly came. If you touched me anymore, we wouldn't be able to hide what we were doing. So I held your hand down and got under your skirt. Because I could make you come. I wanted to make you come—"

I gasped, so turned on.

"I knew it was a bad idea," he whispered, "but I couldn't stop."

"I couldn't either," I told him. "I never wanted to stop."

I reached for him, and he jerked back, pulling my hair, pulling me into him.

"We got caught," he said through clenched teeth. "And it was my fault. Everything that happened was my fault."

His hands in my hair clenched, and I swallowed a moan.

"The Pastor—"

"Tommy, stop."

"I can't," he whispered into my face. "Seven years and I can't stop seeing what that man did to you."

"He didn't do anything."

"Beth."

We both flinched at the use of my name. Like we were being dragged around by these memories.

"He scared me," I told him. "And he would have

done something evil and heinous, but you stopped him. All of you coming in like that. You guys stopped him."

He looked away, detangling his fingers from my hair, the tiny strands caught and stung. I grabbed his hands and held them there, in my hair, against my skin. Forcing him to see me. Hear me.

"Part of the reason," I said, "that I have any perspective on what happened that night is because of you and the art room."

He pulled his hands away, and I let them go. His cheeks flushed. His breath heaved.

"You showed me it was supposed to be something sweet and exciting and mutual."

He stood up like he was going to run.

"No." I stood in his way. "I get to say this, Tommy. I need to say this, and I think you need to hear it."

"I don't want…"

"I'm okay," I told him. "The marks that man left on my soul are far more shallow than the marks he left on yours, and you can stop worrying about it. Worrying about me."

He was turned away, and with my trembling fingers I cupped his face, turning him toward me. "What we did together in the art room was important, Tommy. Real important. And I never forgot it and I never forgot you."

"You should have," he said. "I did everything I could to forget you."

It hurt. It was a knife slipped between my ribs right into my heart.

"Every garbage pill I took. All the poison I put in my veins."

"No, Tommy," I breathed.

"It was to forget you."

He stepped away.

"I never wanted to see you again," he said.

I turned aside, the distance between us a cavern, and it still wasn't enough. I walked to the far side of the room, my back to him. I could hear the sound of his hands over his face, through his hair.

I had thought that his memories had been like mine. Fond. Hot. I never expected that they hurt him. Couldn't stand that they did. He took drugs to forget me. To erase us. Because the memories were worse than the poison of the drug.

Oh God. I mean…

"I need… I just need a little sleep," he said, sounding so weary and broken. This big man at the end of his rope.

"Of course," I said, all business, jumping away from the land mines between us onto safer ground. "Lie down. The sheets are clean. I changed the pillow—"

"I'm gonna close my eyes for a second," he said in

the coldest voice ever. "And then I'll take you home."

"Home," I breathed. The word was pretty fucking foreign. I had an apartment on La Brea. A one-room place with a den that I bought with my Katy Perry makeup money. I hadn't been back there in almost seven months.

Was that home?

"Wherever you want to go," he said, not looking at me. He crawled into the bed, lying down on his stomach, and Pest jumped up on the bed with him, curling up in the small of his giant spine.

Pest faced me, her snaggletooth out—giving me fair warning that I shouldn't get close.

"It's okay," I told the dog and perhaps myself. "He's safe from me."

That wasn't totally the case. It seemed that even my being here hurt him. And I'd known that, but I'd ignored it.

"Well, whose fault is that?" I muttered. It's not like I kidnapped him.

But even that situation wasn't completely clear. He'd kidnapped me, yes, but at the same time he'd saved me in some capacity. I woke up this morning feeling better than I had in ages.

I felt like myself, and that was thanks to Tommy.

Nothing, it seemed, with Tommy was completely clear.

My body curled in on itself with the bitter sweetness of all the memories. The pleasure pain of recalling them, and that he only felt the pain was a blow I didn't know how to handle. So I decided not to handle it. Not right now, anyway. Instead I would do what I always did when the past began to tie me in knots—I thought of the future.

I thought about the people I should call and the life I needed to get back to. The dream I had to repair. If I could. Could I?

Did I want to?

For a second, white-hot and awful, I wished for Dr. John and his bullshit medicine so the stress couldn't touch me. The shame and regret could be put away.

But I sat still and I let it wash over me, I let my shame and my regret fill me. I forced myself to feel it. To just sit there and feel every awful inch of it. Every crushing ounce of it.

I wanted to cry it was so awful. I wanted to scream. And to run.

But I didn't. I'd made that mistake already. I closed my eyes, and I did what I did when I was a kid in that hypnotherapist's office. I took all that shit, and I added it to my armor. I took all my weakness, and I made it into a strength.

I wasn't going down that road with the drugs again.

I had to figure this out. I had to figure *me* out.

If the cost of this music career was losing myself to drugs, it was too high. I'd go back to makeup. I'd go back to YouTube. I'd do something…anything other than what I'd been doing.

And the thought, the realization was like the best armor I'd ever had.

I had choices. They weren't easy, but they so rarely were. But they were there, past others' expectations of me and my own pride.

There were people I really needed to get in touch with, but I didn't have my phone.

Tommy's phone was charging on the floor, plugged into an outlet by the fire. I went over there and unplugged it. There was no password on it. His screen just opened up and I saw all his texts from…*oh my God, Simon.*

At once I was buffeted by memories of the intense boy with the eyes that could break your heart. He'd held himself so far away from the rest of us, studying all the time.

But he'd broken in that door when the Pastor tried to rape me.

How you doing? Simon had texted. I thought about how I was invading Tommy's privacy and should really put down the phone. But then I reminded myself that he'd kidnapped me.

Kidnapping trumped texting privacy.

Ready to be out of here, Tommy had texted back. *How is the lice?*

Gone. Where are you going to go? You can't go back to your place. Not with Bates looking for you.

Thought I'd stay with you a few days.

I don't know, Tommy. If Bates is looking for you, he'll look here too.

Good point.

Tommy didn't have anywhere to go. I wondered what he'd do if I invited him to my apartment. I wondered what he'd do if I reminded him of that grandfather who lived just south of Santa Barbara.

Well, I knew what he'd do: he'd drop me off, slam the door and drive away and never see me again.

How is Beth? Simon wrote.

Better. She'll be fine in another day.

Yeah. But how is she?

The texts ended there. I swallowed against the lump in my throat. It wasn't surprising how badly he wanted to be away from me, and I didn't blame him. I really didn't. I just had no idea I was such torture for him.

I opened the phone app and called my manager, Sherman. It rang three times and went to voice mail. Which felt...ominous.

"Sherman," I said, my voice low, my eyes on Tommy in the bed to see if I was being too loud and waking him up. But he didn't even twitch. The guy was out.

"It's Jada. I'm calling to let you know that I'm better and that I will be back in the city probably tomorrow afternoon at the latest. Can we have a meeting? Talk about how to salvage Europe? Let me know. You can call me back at this number."

After I hung up, I watched the phone for a few more minutes, waiting for, if nothing else, a text letting me know he was in a meeting and he'd call me back as soon as he could. But no reply came back.

Demi Lovato had told me stories about what happened after her crash a few years ago, how hard she'd had to work to get back in the game.

And I was ready to do that work. I was. I just wasn't sure how.

And my body still had the craving for the stress-free life of Dr. John's medicine bag.

My stomach roared, and I stood up from the chair and looked at the desk in the corner where Tommy had all our provisions set up. Crackers and oranges. Water and Gatorade.

I remembered how I used to give him my lunch. How he'd try and refuse, but he was so hungry all the time and in the end he'd take half my sandwich or the cheese string. His favorites were Doritos and those little baby carrots.

All at once I wanted to bring him Doritos and baby carrots. And frankly, my body wasn't interested in oranges anymore. I wanted food. Real food.

I found the keys to the car in his coat pocket as well as a small stack of twenty-dollar bills. I took two, and when I opened the door, Pest looked up at me, her ears perked.

"I can't, Pest," I said. If I took her with me and he woke up, he'd be upset.

And I was not going to be in the business of upsetting Tommy.

It would seem I'd done enough of that. Without even trying.

17

Tommy

I WOKE UP slowly, piece by piece, the fog thick in my head. My body felt like it was carved from stone. Heavy and clumsy.

"Move, Pest," I muttered, shifting my hips so the dog would jump off the spot on my back where she liked to sleep. Why I encouraged that, I had no idea. Well, that wasn't true. It was from the drug days, when I was putting shit in my body to forget all the shit that was in my head.

I let her sleep on me so I wouldn't feel like I was floating away.

Pest yipped but hopped off me, coming up on the bed to lick at my nose.

"Good morning to you too," I said and rubbed her whole head with my hand, which for some reason she seemed to love.

I rolled over, staring up at the wooden beams of the ceiling of the cottage. I knew between one breath and the next that she wasn't here. I knew without looking that she was gone.

The air was just air. The room was just a room. There was nothing electric or magic or waiting about any of it.

Sitting up, I confirmed it. The room was empty. The chair, the cold fireplace, the stash of food on the desk.

I had no fucking right to be surprised. I said some seriously mean shit to her. Of course she left. I groaned, the memories of what I said to her echoing in my brain.

Why did I do that? I wondered.

But I knew why. Because I was scared to say what I really wanted to say. When she'd been looking at me in the bathroom, talking about sex like it was nothing. Like it was a casual thing we could do and forget about, I'd been paralyzed with embarrassment.

Because there was nothing casual about me and sex.

And my instinct was to push her away, to make her stop wanting me like that, instead of telling her why I couldn't fucking deal with her wanting me like that.

"Beth?" I said, looking at the shut door of the bathroom. "Beth, you still here?" I stood up and knocked on the door. There was no answer, so I turned the doorknob, easing it open with my fist, wondering what it was exactly that I wanted to find.

What I wanted to feel.

Happy she was gone?

Happy that she'd stayed?

The room was empty. The towel she'd used hung on the rack beside the shower. I touched the edge of it and found it damp and forced myself not to smell it. The sink was splattered with water, strands of her long hair clinging to the porcelain.

I drove her away.

And all at once I was…fucking crushed.

Truly fucking crushed.

She was gone. And it was over.

The part of myself that I'd been ignoring for the last seventy-two hours, the feelings I'd been shoving away or ignoring altogether, they swamped me.

I'd driven her away and I hated it.

That was it. The last time I'd see her. The last time I'd have her in my life, and I'd done what? What exactly? Ignored her? Hurt her on purpose? So she'd stop saying those things to me? Stop looking at me like I was something delicious she wanted to eat?

What kind of fucking coward was I?

The worst kind. The kind that made a woman feel bad because I couldn't get a grip on my own feelings for her. My own fucking memories.

I acted as if that shit with the Pastor happened to

me.

"Goddamn it," I muttered. She'd been here. *Here.* In this place, with her freckles and her beauty, and I'd pretended like I didn't give a shit. I couldn't even stand talking to her because I was an idiot.

A fucking virgin. Who didn't know how to go about not being one.

Loss gutted me.

I crossed the room and grabbed my phone. Simon would fucking never let me hear the end of this. He'd be ruthless. And I pretty much deserved ruthless.

On my phone I saw there'd been an outgoing call to a number I didn't recognize, and I hit redial. Two rings and an outgoing message kicked in.

"This is Sherman Bliss. Leave a message and I'll get back to you. If this is an emergency, call my assistant, Jason, at—" I hung up. She must have called her manager.

That made sense. She had to be getting herself back to her life. She had responsibilities. Obligations.

God. She was a worldwide pop star. Of course she'd left.

Of course she left me. I barely even talked to her. I fucking kidnapped her.

Rubbing my hand over my face, getting rid of the last of the grit and the sleep in my eyes, I shoved my feet in my boots.

She probably took my truck too.

Simon was going to *love* picking me up out here. It would give him so many hours to ream me out for letting the girl I'd put in the center of my life like some kind of sun I orbited, leave me.

Without touching her again.

Kissing her again.

I yanked open the door only to see the gray truck pull into the spot between two pine trees that framed the cottage. She saw me through the windshield and smiled. She'd bought sunglasses, big black ones, and she'd put on makeup and her hair was up in a bun on the top of her head.

My body buzzed with relief. I put my hand on the door jamb because I was lightheaded with it.

She wasn't gone. She didn't leave.

Another chance. Another few hours.

To answer the questions I'd been asking myself for seven years.

All at once I decided not to fucking waste it. No, I was going to make the most of these hours. Make the most of her.

"Hey," she said, hopping out of the truck. She had grocery bags and a McDonald's bag and a fountain pop cup that I imagined she had full of Diet Coke. Because she'd loved Diet Coke with an intensity that couldn't just go away. "I picked up some more food," she said, holding up the bags like maybe I hadn't seen them.

I saw them. I just didn't care. I wanted to hurl those bags into the bushes and pull off those ridiculous clothes I'd bought her so I could see her body.

"Hamburgers," she said as I continued to stare at her. "Doritos and baby carrots. You used to love those things, so I took a stab that you still did." She stopped in front of me because I was barring the door, and instead of jumping out of her way, I shifted just a little so she had to squeeze by me. It was a dick move.

But I was feeling like a dick.

Her lips—painted bright red—parted like she knew what I was doing, and fuck, she probably did. In this, we'd shared a mind. A brain. I'd known as a kid how to touch this woman in a way I never knew how to touch anyone else.

For just a second doubt rippled through me, but I ignored it. I'd been a virgin then and I'd still gotten her off, pushed up against a bulletin board in an art room.

Here I was going to lay her out on that bed and fucking worship her.

Virgin or not.

She turned sideways, brushing against me, sliding through the space I'd left for her, and I felt her shoulder, her breast. The hair in a top knot on her head brushed my chin. Her eyes were on mine every single inch.

I could barely breathe.

The air was suddenly kerosene, waiting for a match.

Once she was in the room, her back to me, I shut the door. The sound of the lock clicking home made both of us drag in a breath. She'd tied her T-shirt into a knot in the small of her back, pulling the fabric up to reveal a slice of skin between her leggings and the shirt.

She had a freckle near her spine that I could not look away from.

Where else did she have freckles? That was a question I'd had for seven years that suddenly, urgently needed answering.

She turned, her sunglasses still on, hiding her eyes, and that was okay with me. That was…easier for me. While I watched, sucking in shallow breaths, my dick pounding against the zipper of my jeans, she put the cup and the keys to the truck down on the table, and I reached out and trapped her hand there.

I watched myself do it from a million miles away. Like it was me, but not. Her, but not.

I felt like we were strangers, but not.

Please, I thought, *understand what I'm doing so I don't have to say the words. Talking will ruin this.*

I felt her try to move, and I wouldn't let her. And then, that tensile tension in her arm vanished.

She knew what this was. And she wanted it too.

The bags in her other hand hit the floor.

"What do you want, Tommy?" she breathed. So close. So beautiful. With her free hand she took off her glasses and tossed them on the ground. Her eyes, lined in black liner, raked over me.

And mine raked over her.

"You," I said, so raw I was practically inside out. "Just once."

She laughed low in her throat. "You have a few questions you want answered, do you?" she asked.

"Don't you?"

"God yes."

She stepped forward until she was nearly touching me. It took my inhale for my chest to brush hers. I exhaled and our bodies retreated. She inhaled and we touched. Exhaled and retreated.

We each did it again. And then again. Breathing each other in, in turns. Finally it wasn't enough and I stepped toward her, and my cock pressed against her stomach and she pushed against me. Her breasts and belly imprinted on my skin.

"One time," she said. "One time and we go back to our lives and get on with things. I'm going to forget you, Tommy. And you're going to forget me."

I doubted it, but I wasn't going to argue. Not with my dick pushed up against the tight muscles of her stomach. Not with her breath, sweet from the pop and the candy she'd eaten, making me crazy.

"I'm serious, Tommy," she said as if she could read my mind. "I don't want to be hurt anymore, and I really, really don't want to hurt you anymore. Promise you'll forget me."

"I promise," I said, because when threatened with the idea of hurting her, I'd agree to anything to stop that. "I'll forget you, right after I fuck you."

She laughed, which was the point. "Maybe I'll fuck you, Tommy. Maybe that's how this plays out."

I shook my head. I wasn't that boy anymore, following her lead, happy just to have her notice me. I was a man. And this was going to have to go my way. Or it wouldn't work at all.

"Take down your hair," I said.

She looked at me, puzzled.

"I want it down." Beth had her hair up. Jada would take it down.

Jada. Not Beth.

That's how I'd do this and let her go tomorrow. That's how I'd do this and not fall apart.

Jada. Not Beth.

With her free hand she pulled out the black rubber band that held her hair in place, and the damp blue and green and pink hair fell down around her shoulders.

"It's different—" she started, but I shook my head.

"No," I told her. "No talking."

Beth had been a talker, constantly chatting. I'd loved it. Her voice had chased out so many of the demons. So many of the fears. I couldn't let that voice back in.

She shut her mouth with a snap, her eyebrows furrowed.

"My way," I said, "or no."

"You've changed."

I hadn't, but it was all right to let her think so.

"So have you."

"What if I want to talk dirty?" she asked, tilting her head, playing with me, taunting me, turning me inside out. "What if I want to tell you to take out your dick? Or to suck my tits? What if I want to tell you to fuck me harder? Or slower? What if I want to tell you how good your cock feels…"

I kissed her. I kissed her to shut her up. To keep those words from filling my head with every one of those visions. I kept her hand pinned to the table, but with my other hand I grabbed the back of her neck and held her still while I kissed her.

While I kissed her the way I'd dreamed of kissing her.

Nothing careful. Nothing shy. I opened her lips with mine, and I let myself into her. I kissed her like she was already mine.

Mine.

She gasped and melted against me, her free hand grabbing my shoulder, her nails digging into my skin, and maybe she was thinking the same thing. That I was hers.

That we'd agreed to this moment years ago.

She tasted just the way I remembered. Her mouth was warm and damp, and I wanted to die there. I wanted to push my cock between her lips into her mouth.

Fuck. This was going to be over fast.

She pushed her stomach against me, trapping my cock between our bellies, and she pushed and retreated just a little, with every breath again. Fucking me between us. I clenched my hand, pulling her hair, and she groaned and gasped, pulling away from my mouth to breathe.

Oh. Right. Breathing.

Her lipstick was smeared, her mouth wet from my mouth and I loved it.

"Fuck," she breathed. "Tommy."

I bent my lips to her neck, kissing her there. The hard ridge of her throat and tendons, the velvet skin that covered all of it. She pulled herself up on her tiptoes, using me as leverage, her breasts against my chest. Her legs against my legs.

"I need," she breathed, and it was all so familiar. So

familiar for a second I couldn't stand it. I wanted to pull away. I wanted to run. My body went still, and she writhed against me once more and then stopped.

"Oh no," she breathed, shaking her head at me, her eyes all blissed out. "No. You can't fucking go all Tommy on me now. We're finishing this."

She yanked her hand free from my grip. Dumb, I stood there as she whipped off that ridiculous wolf T-shirt that I'd bought her and she made look better than it ever should, and beneath that her bra, and then she toed off her shoes and put her hands to the waist of her leggings.

"No," I breathed, my hand out, brushing the tender skin of her tummy. The fragile bones of her rib cage. "Just. Wait."

I was taking her in, soaking her in. Burning the memory of this woman bared to the waist for me into my brain.

She was beautiful perfection. Her waist was curved, her belly button had a dark scar where she'd once had a piercing. Her collarbone, the thin strength of her arms. The curve of her neck. All of it beautiful.

And her breasts, with their dark brown nipples, answered another question.

Beth had amazing tits.

"Done staring?" she asked, her chin up.

"No."

"Take off your shirt."

I did, without thinking. My body was its own thing. A tool, like a jackhammer or a saw. I did nothing to it besides work it to the bone nearly every single day.

"Jesus," she breathed. "Tommy. Look at you."

"I'm looking at you," I said.

"You're..." She ran her hands from my shoulders down my arms to my hands. And then she did it again, only along my chest, across the muscles of my stomach. Over and over again, she touched me, top to bottom, as if mapping me. "You're so fucking beautiful."

There was nothing to say, so I slipped my hands around the bare skin of her waist and she gasped. Twitched.

Fuck. My hands. They were so goddamned wrecked. "I'm sorry," I said, pulling back.

I almost told her then, that I didn't know what I was doing. But the truth, that I barely let myself think about, was embarrassing. Ridiculous. I couldn't even imagine telling her—that other than a few minor exceptions, I hadn't touched another woman like this.

Ever.

And no, I wasn't joking.

She would have questions, and I had no easy answer for those questions except that she'd moved on and I'd stayed stuck.

"No, no, no." She grabbed my hands again, and this time put them on her breasts. "Yes," she gasped as if she was answering her own questions. I covered her breasts with my palms and the rough skin on her tender flesh felt like a sacrilege to me, but she seemed to like it.

I gripped her. Squeezed. And she moaned. Cried out. Like I was perfect. Like my touch was just right.

"More," she begged.

Growling, I put one arm around her back and picked her up off her feet, turning her so her back was against the door, and I leaned into her, keeping her there. She wrapped her legs around my waist, her arms around my neck, and I put my mouth to hers and devoured her.

We kissed like we were dying. Like an antidote for pain was in each other's mouths.

We kissed like it was the first time and the last time all at once.

My cock felt the damp heat between her legs, and I rode that spot, arching into her so hard I was sure it had to hurt. But every time I pushed, she arched back at me, a push and pull that made me crazy. Wild.

She shoved her hand between our bodies, her fingers tugging at the button of my jeans, and they were old and soft and came undone without any effort on her part. The button, then the zipper, and then her hand slipped inside my boxers to find the stiff, hard length of my cock.

"There's a question answered," she breathed against me, smiling through lips covered in smeared lipstick. Her mouth was swollen, and I'd done that too. "You're big, Tommy. You're big all the way around."

She stroked me, her thumb slipping over the top, finding the cum leaking out that I couldn't control. Wasn't even sure how I would try. She brought her thumb up to her mouth, her gaze on mine. Burning into my brain.

She put her thumb in her mouth, tasting me, and I leaned forward, kissing the taste from her tongue, her thumb.

"Fuck," she breathed and her hand was back between my legs, jacking me slowly. I felt the orgasm rising up out of my blood, a ball of tension in my lower back. My feet feeling numb. And I pulled away from her.

"What are you doing?" she asked.

"I'm not coming in your hand."

"I want you to come in my hand," she said and licked my throat. Sucked the skin of my neck into her mouth, hard enough that I gasped. Hard enough I'd have a mark. "It's like an art-room alternate reality. Where I get what I want."

"I'll give you what you want," I said.

I tore the leggings off her. They were cheap and I was strong as fuck and they made a sound in the quiet between us that I could tell she liked. Every time I worried I was going too far, it seemed it wasn't far enough.

Not for Beth.

Jada.

I tore the leggings until they hung off one ankle and I put one arm on the wall beside her head and the other hand between her legs. Where she was unbearably hot.

And had considerably less hair than when we were in high school.

My fingers slipped right over her, her folds slippery. Wet. My fingers were coated in her. Drenched.

"Spread your legs," I said, and she did, breathing in great sobs. I cupped her in my palm. The whole of her sex in my hand. I pushed against her clit and watched her eyes roll back in her head.

When we were kids, I'd made her come like this. Pressure and pressure until she came apart on my fingers and I'd felt like I'd given her something real and precious and important.

But this time, I pushed my fingers inside of her. One and then another. Another.

And she took them all, asked for more.

And I pressed my thumb against the hard knot of

her clit.

"Jesus," she cried, pulling at my hair, scratching at my neck. She was taut and strained. Every muscle clamped and wild, and I turned my head and captured her nipple in my mouth, pulling and pulling until I heard her gasp, like the sound of a lock unlocking, and she went to pieces against me.

She cried out and jerked, twisting between me and the door.

"Tommy," she sighed, her body fluid and soft. I took my fingers out of her, away from her, the air cold against my skin where I was wet with her. I could smell her, musky and sweet. I remembered the smell from years ago, how I'd carried it on my skin for a day.

I put my fingers to my face, breathing her in. I licked my thumb, where it had been against her clit, and her eyes, watching me, opened wide. I put a finger in my mouth, sucking off the taste of her. I put my other hand between her legs, and when my fingers were wet enough with her, I put them to her mouth. Wiped them against her lips until she opened them and we were tasting her together.

Her eyes locked on mine, and I saw the way she was after this, the way she was living this, like there were no other moments between us but this one.

And I was so fucking envious of that, my teeth hurt. I was envious of the way she looked right at me without shame or worry or fear. Like the intimacy of this, of each of us sucking her cum off my fingers was bearable to her.

Because it was unbearable to me.

I looked away.

I felt more than heard the sigh of her disappointment, and I could have told her that my whole life had been about avoiding these moments. Avoiding getting close to anyone, because it ultimately turned to shit. It was the first lesson I ever learned, alone in that apartment waiting for my mother to come home.

But I wasn't ever talking about that. Not ever.

"Tommy," she breathed, "what's wrong?"

Instead of answering, I kissed her. I kissed her with everything I'd never said and wanted to. Everything I never said and should have.

I remembered suddenly what I'd really wanted in that classroom. What I'd thought about over and over again until I'd worn myself raw in the bathroom. I stepped away from her, my hand at her waist, keeping her against the door when she would have pulled away from it.

"Stay there," I said.

"I don't want to." She pushed against me, and I pushed her right back. Keeping her where I wanted her. She tried again, harder, rearranging the boundaries of this thing between us, and I, clumsy and unsure, pushed her back harder. She gasped, smiling. Her eyes wide and delighted.

She fucking loved this.

Well, if rough was fun for her, I could be rough.

All I was, was rough.

I kicked her legs out wider. "Move from this spot," I said, "and I won't let you come."

Her breath was ragged, her hands in fists at her sides as she waited for what I was going to do to her. I wondered if she thought I'd hurt her, because that wasn't going to happen. I was rough. Not...that. Maybe?

But the not knowing was turning this thing between us into something razor-sharp, both of us being cut in ways we liked, so I kept my mouth shut. I put my hands to her waist, holding her against the door, my fingertips biting into her flesh, her skin bowing beneath the pressure. I could feel the muscles under there.

She gasped.

And then I went to my knees.

"Tommy," she breathed.

"This is what I want," I said, breathing over her pussy, dusky pink and swollen. Wet. "Are you going to give me what I want?" I asked her.

She nodded; I felt the movement in the muscles of her stomach. Her name rose to my lips, but I swallowed it down and leaned forward, pressing a kiss to the small bit of hair on her pussy. I licked her, finding the hidden seam that hid all her secrets.

All her secrets I wanted. I shifted, finding the right place, and this time when I licked, the point of my tongue went right through that seam. Right into heart of her. She gasped. Twitched. I picked up her foot and put it on my knee, opening her up.

"Yes," I said. I held her open with my thumbs, pulling the skin taut until she winced. I kissed her in apology. Licking the folds, finding her clit, the hole of her pussy. My hand slid beneath her leg, stroking the hard muscle of her thighs, the sleek skin of her ass. I gripped her in my palm and squeezed. I squeezed until she cried out and jerked forward into my mouth.

I held her there against me, and I fucked her with my face. My mouth and tongue. I licked her and kissed her and sucked her down. My fingers were all over her. She was shaking and crying, her fingers on my skull, over my hair, squeezing my head so hard it should have hurt but that was the nature of this pleasure between us.

We needed it to hurt.

I sucked on her clit, pulling it into my mouth while I fucked my fingers into her, and she came for a second time. A wild gush against my palm and even that wasn't enough. It would never be enough. I kept going until she came again, and when she pushed me away, I was so into it, I ignored her. Eager for more. Ready to make her come again and again.

"Please, Tommy," she breathed. "It hurts."

I let go of her. Sat back on my ass, my hand too late to catch my weight. I felt like I'd spent the last hour jackhammering. I was numb and shaking and my body didn't feel right and my hands felt like they were alive and twitchy with nerves coming back to life.

"I'm sorry," I said, looking up at her where she stood at the door.

Fuck. Me. Like forever.

She was naked, and her hair was a wild cloud and her eyes were full of fire and desire and she was looking at me like I was hers.

"Sensitive," she said, her hand over her pussy, like some sham portrait of modesty. Fuck. I could come just looking at her. "That's all."

I didn't know that was a thing, but I wasn't going to tell her that.

"Get down here," I said, pulling her onto the ground with me. She split her legs over mine, her hand back at my cock, now leaking cum like a hose with a hole in it.

"Ask me to suck your dick," she said, watching me through her hair.

"Suck my dick."

"Ask me."

"I told you." I pushed my jeans down past my ass, the floor cold against my overhot skin.

"What if I fuck you instead?" she asked.

I shook my head. Not... I mean, it was fucking ridiculous to think it, but I wasn't ready. I was twenty-three years old and I wasn't...ready.

"We don't have a condom," I said.

She shook her head, the black lace of her hair parting over her creamy shoulders. "You always were the reasonable one," she said, and without saying anything else, she gripped my cock in her hand and bent over me. Her hair hid what she was doing, and that was okay. I was strung so tight if I watched her lipstick-smeared lips taking me, I'd fucking pop.

I felt the heat of her breath, the dampness when she opened her mouth over the head of my cock and then—

"Fuck. God!" I groaned. And then it didn't matter if I came in an instant; I had to see it. I had to watch her. I gathered up her hair in my rough hands, probably pulling it, but I didn't care and she didn't either. We were blown out with lust. We were numb to anything but this fucking fire between us.

"Yes," I breathed, watching her mouth stretch wide, slipping down over the ramrod-hard length of me. The veins and tendons were slick with her spit. She took me fast and slow, her hand gripping the base of me, holding me still. "Suck me." The words were barely breaths out of my mouth. Barely thoughts in my brain. But she liked them. I could tell, the hum of her pleasure reverberating against me.

Years ago she'd begged me to talk. To tell her things, and I'd thought I had nothing to offer her, this brilliant star. And so I'd said nothing.

But these words. These filthy sex words. I had them. I had a lot of them, pent up and kept inside for seven years. If she wanted these words, she could have them.

"Jada—"

She flinched at the use of her other name, and for a second I thought she was going to stop. So I kept talking. Like my filthy mouth could keep her here.

"Suck my cock, baby. Oh my God. Yes. Yes. Just like that. You look so fucking good like this."

It worked, and she took me deep, my cock disappearing, and I tried to arch up onto my heels, the pleasure too much, it felt like electricity in my veins, and when she let me go, it was with a gasp and pop. Her eyes were watering, black mascara running down the side of her face, her lips swollen and smeared.

"You are so beautiful."

"You like this look," she said with a smile that told me she knew how fucking sexy she looked. How dirty.

I wanted to tell her that I liked her. Every way she was. Every way she looked.

But she bent down to me again, licking me and sucking my head. Her fingers playing with my balls. Her fingertip brushed the crease of my ass, and I flinched away.

"No ass play, Tommy?"

"I want to come down your throat."

Her cheeks went pink, her eyes went wide and when she bent over me again, she meant fucking business. It was heat and pressure and suction and I didn't last. Couldn't last.

"I'm going to come," I said, and she held me deep in her mouth as the orgasm rolled over me, took me under like a wave. I came in spurts, wild and messy, and she stayed with me the whole way. Not letting me go.

Because I was begging her not to.

18

Beth

"DON'T LET ME GO. *Fuck. Beth. Please. Don't let me go.*"

I mean, they were just words, I told myself, leaning away from him, wiping at my mouth. They didn't mean anything. Sex talk. That was all.

I just wasn't sure I believed it.

Because in that moment—vulnerable and outside himself—he called me Beth.

Everything felt…different. My skin felt shaky over my bones, like it didn't quite fit me.

My lips were sore. My pussy too. I was…sensitive all over.

I pushed my hair out of my face and looked at him. Really looked at him. Soaking him in as a whole and then again in pieces like he was artwork I was going to recreate.

"You okay?" His fingertips touched my shoulder.

"I wish—"

He shook his head. "Careful," he whispered. "That's dangerous."

"I know. But let me wish. Just…just for this second. For a minute. Give me a minute to wish."

He exhaled, his fingers pushing the hair out of my eyes, and nodded. "Go ahead, then. Wish."

"I wish I'd been able to find you seven years ago."

His smile was tight, like he was holding it in. Like he didn't dare wish.

"I wish I hadn't hurt you so much. I'd give anything to not have hurt you."

"Not everything hurts," he said, smiling and running his hand down my bare hip.

"But most of it does."

He didn't argue.

"I wish we'd just met," I said. "That we didn't have any of this shit behind us."

He smiled, crooked and endearing. "How would the two of us have met?" he asked.

"We could have met at a party."

"I don't go to parties."

"A bar—"

"I'm a recovering addict, Beth. I go to one bar, because they let my dog come in. I drink one beer. I'm not…a good time."

"I think you are."

"Don't lie to yourself. You know you deserve more

than me."

"I wish you didn't believe that." My heart chipped at the edges. "You go," I said. "Tell me something you wish."

"I don't wish, Beth. I can't."

"Everyone wishes. Everyone wants something better than what they have."

He shook his head, the silence thick and suffocating.

"But," he said. "I like that you wish. Wish something for both of us."

I closed my eyes with a painful melancholy too sharp to even bear.

It took me a second to get past the lump in my throat.

"We could have met at the park," I said. "Pest would have gotten loose from her leash." "She does that sometimes," he murmured.

"Of course she does," I whispered.

"And she would have led me straight towards you."

"I'd grab her, and when you come running up I would have said something very clever like 'does this belong to you?'"

"And I would say something really clever like, 'want to get some coffee?'"

"I would say yes."

He stopped stroking my hair, and the air around us

grew colder.

"Tell me," I said.

"What?"

"Tell me why these wishes can't come true."

Remind me why we can't be together; that's what I was asking him. And he knew it.

"Because you are fucking magic, Beth. And I'm stone. You have a life to get back to. You have people counting on you. A career. You've got some ground to make up after the last few weeks. And there's no place for me in that. And I don't want to be the thing that keeps you from being what you should be."

I pushed my face into the skin beneath his armpit where he smelled the most like him.

"And I…" he said. "I live in a shitty one-bedroom apartment in the worst neighborhood in the city. I have a really bad guy who is going to come after me at some point, and Carissa, who—if she finds out I touched you—has threatened to have my balls. Tell me what part of that life you want?"

His life made me sad. And angry.

"I just…I want you."

"You have me. And I have you. One night."

"And then…?"

"It's over and you know that. Right? Beth? Tell me you know that."

"I know that."

We both took a second to swallow the truth.

"We're not a fairy tale," I said, and he nodded, his face all folded up, like all his thoughts were put away. "I used to think we were."

"So did I," he said and that was a comfort, at least. We'd felt the same way for a while there. And that had enough sweetness in it to last a while.

I found my underwear next to his hip and slipped it on while he pulled up his pants. Neither of us looking at each other. I hadn't noticed how cold the room was when his body had been pressed to mine. But now my skin rose up in goose bumps.

"Here," he said, his voice so different from what it had been a few minutes ago while he'd told me to suck his dick. I was sore, my body exhausted, my head a mess, but the memory of his voice saying those words turned something over in my body. And would for a long time. Maybe forever.

"You told me to suck your dick," I said and then giggled. I actually giggled and he actually blushed and the feelings in my heart were sharp enough to cut.

"I did."

"That's going in the spank bank, Tommy. Top-shelf spank bank, right there."

"Oh my God," he muttered like I was just too much.

I put the shirt on, the bra gone. The leggings… in

ruins. I held them up in my hands, torn in pieces.

What am I supposed to do now?

Behind me I heard Tommy getting to his feet, and I turned in time to see him standing up, his back to me. The skin of his back was so pale compared to his forearms and the back of his neck, so maybe that's why I could see the faded scars, no longer pink but silver almost, along his spine and sides. Like stretch marks. Physical proof of growing pains.

"Tommy," I sighed.

He turned and caught me staring, read maybe on my face what I was thinking.

"It was a long time ago," he said and shrugged into his shirt, the scars hidden but there. Always there. I'd never not see them.

"Not that long," I said.

He took a deep breath, and in the silence before he said something, we heard the scuttle of paper across the floor and Pest came trotting across the room with a cheeseburger wrapper in her mouth.

"Dinner!" I cried.

Tommy snagged Pest and pulled the wrapper from her mouth. "I should have warned you. Cheeseburgers are her favorite."

"Well, she got her fair share of them," I said, picking up the McDonald's bag. She'd eaten two, the third one she hadn't gotten to in the bottom of the bag. It was cold but edible. I handed it to him, trying not to laugh.

"It's yours," he said. "You're probably starving."

I was. I was starving. "You probably are too," I said.

He picked up the other bag, which had the Doritos and carrots in it. "This will work for me."

He smiled, showing me the teenage Tommy's delight in Doritos and baby carrots.

Still his favorite.

All at once I couldn't believe this was the end.

"I have so much I want to say," I told him and he was immediately shaking his head, but I just kept on talking. "And so much I want you to say. So much I want to hear—"

"Why?"

I blinked, stunned by the question. "What do you mean, why?"

"Talking isn't going to change anything." He jerked his thumb back at the floor where we'd had sex and sketched out our alternate reality life.

"It might make the memories we have of each other hurt less," I said, feeling unbelievably shy considering what we'd just done to each other. "Because I don't really think it's our future keeping us apart. It's the past. And how we don't talk about it. But we're reminded of it every time we look at each other. That's the real truth of why we can't be together. Because our past makes it hurt too much."

He knew I was right; I could tell just by looking at him. Just by the clench of his jaw and the way he kept making fists with his hands like he was holding onto something he wanted to let go of.

"We never talked about your parents. My mom. What we did to get to St. Joke's. We talked all the time, but we never talked about that. We wrote notes and knocked on the walls, and we created these wishes we couldn't say out loud. Everything we never put into words, it's sitting right here in this room. Between us like walls."

He blinked at me, those blue eyes seeing me as clearly as I saw him. My mother, the last seven years, that night, the scars on his back, the man that had him kidnap me—all those things were in our way.

And I felt, for just one second, that if he asked, I'd answer. I'd tell him everything. I'd use my whole body and all my strength to clear out all the things between us so we could breathe fresh air. So we could make each other feel good, without making each other feel bad.

I opened my mouth just as he said, "I can't."

I nodded. "I know."

Because I did know. It was a truth I understood down in my bones.

Our complicated future was nothing compared to

our complicated past.

He shrugged at my silence, and I felt the naked length of my legs, my breasts without a bra. My hair like a sex-tossed cloud around my head. I felt every single way he'd stripped me and changed me and then…didn't want me.

"Tomorrow," he said, "I'm going to take you wherever you want to go and it's over."

We just kept nodding at each other like idiots, because what could we do?

And everything we didn't talk about cluttered the room like ghosts and monsters and animals let loose in the wilds of our lives. He saw them too, he felt them too but he'd rather not deal with them.

We'd part ways and those ghosts would vanish and the monsters wouldn't be as scary and the animals would become our pets again, like they had been for seven years. Because we weren't together, constantly reminding each other of everything we wished we could forget.

Pest scratched at the door and whined. "I better take her out," he said and opened the door, letting in even cooler night air. "And I'll find you some new pants."

And he was gone.

19

Tommy

IT'S NOT LIKE I set out to stay a virgin. It became a habit I didn't know how to break, like smoking. Or chewing my nails. When Simon and I first got the apartment, I was too beat up for a few months, and then we were too busy trying to just keep a roof over our heads and food in our mouths to even think about girls.

When Simon left, that's when the drugs started. Most of a year gone to that shit until he came back on summer break, locked me in the apartment, and cleaned me up.

The oranges thing had been his trick.

After that I felt like I had to concentrate on being clean. Being some version of a better me.

And after that…it was just…habit. Being a virgin. Being alone really. Habit coming up with excuses. Habit looking away when a girl looked too long. Habit finding some reason to leave a girl's apartment earlier and earlier until I didn't even go to the apartment. Instead, I went home and watched some shitty video of a girl being tied up and held down and made to come until she begged the guy to stop.

I mean…when I laid it out like that…this virginity thing was pretty fucked-up.

A million years ago Beth asked me in that art room if I'd been waiting for her, and it was a joke. But it wasn't. It wasn't then. And it wasn't now.

I hadn't been waiting for her, but I'd been waiting for something. Waiting to put something away. Us. That night. The person I'd thought I was.

At the truck stop about twenty minutes away from the cottage, I bought her a pair of sweatpants and I grabbed a box of condoms too.

Because I was done with this shit. I was done with living my life like I'd been poured into concrete.

I was done with the ghost of Beth. With the ghosts of both of us.

I was done being lost without her.

Tonight I'd end it all.

Because I couldn't be the guy she wanted.

On the way back everything I wanted to do to her stacked up in my mind. Every fantasy I'd ever had put its hand up to be noticed. By the time I got back to the cottage, I was hard as stone.

I was so hard there was no doubt. No habit to fall

back on.

It was me and her. And it was over tonight.

The door to the cottage opened without a sound. Jada was asleep in the bed, a small lump in the covers. The bell on Pest's collar broke the silence as she pranced in, settling in her spot in front of the fireplace, and Beth sat up, hair rumpled around her face, still streaked with mascara.

She was and always would be the most beautiful woman I'd ever seen.

"Sweatpants," I said, holding them up before putting them down across the back of the chair. And then I put the box on the bedside table—too hard, maybe, because it sounded like a smack in the quiet.

"Condoms," she said and I nodded.

I waited, in part, for her to say no. To say forget it. We'd said some harsh things to each other.

"Only if you still want—"

"Of course I do," she said, not sounding particularly happy about it. "It's always a yes with us, isn't it?"

I sat in the chair and pulled off my boots. Stood and pulled off my shirt. Her lips parted as she breathed, and I imagined I could smell her desire. I could feel it in the air between us. My hands went to the buttons of my jeans, and she pushed the blankets off herself and crawled to the edge of the bed.

"Let me," she said, and I took the three steps toward her and she unbuttoned my jeans, her fingers warm against my stomach. Shocking, in a way. I put my hands against hers, flattening her palms against my belly. Her fingers to my skin.

"What did you do to your hands?" she asked, turning her hands to hold mine. I tried to pull away, so aware of the rough calluses and old scars, but she held on, turning my hands over so we were both looking at the damage.

"For years I worked without gloves. Fucked them up."

"Why would you do that?"

I was silent because silence was where I felt safest. I didn't know how to talk like she wanted me to.

The wolf howling at the moon T-shirt was glowing a little in the semidarkness, and it should have been funny. It was funny. I just couldn't find the air to laugh. It was so big on her, the collar slipped down, revealing her neck, the scrapes from my beard. The place I'd sucked on her skin, leaving behind a red smudge of blood under the surface.

I had one of those on my neck too. We'd left our marks on each other.

"The scars," I said, rubbing my thumbs over the silvery tails of some of them that could still be seen. He'd whipped my hands with something thin and vicious, and the scars had not gone away so I had to do something.

"Covering up old scars with new ones?"

New pain for old pain seemed like a deal I just kept making.

She got up on her knees in front of me, her eyes on mine. She pulled the howling wolf up over her head, tossing it into the darkness at the edge of the lamplight.

I felt the warm, moist breath of her exhale against my shoulder, my neck, the corner of my face, and it wasn't enough. Not nearly enough.

"This is good-bye," she breathed.

I felt myself rising to the surface. The kid I'd been. Her Tommy.

And that was terrifying. Impossible. So I put my hands in her hair, pulling it in my fists, until her head tipped back.

She gasped and I felt the foreignness of us. We were strangers like this.

And that's what I needed.

I needed this to be over.

Beth

TOMMY WAS HARD against my belly and his hands in my hair were rough, his mouth on my neck made me wild and all of that was my favorite flavor. But this was good-bye.

Beth was saying good-bye to Tommy, and I couldn't do it like this. I wanted this to take a long time and I wanted to look into his eyes and I wanted...a lot.

"Stop," I breathed against his lips, and his hands let go of my hair like I'd pulled a switch. He shifted as if to step away, but I put my hands in the open fly of his jeans, holding him where he was.

"You don't like that?" he asked, his eyes looking anywhere but at me.

"I do like it and you know it, but this is good-bye, Tommy."

He was silent and I kissed him. Softly, sweetly. I licked at his lips and I breathed in the smell of his skin and I felt his body under my hands. Long slow kisses that would last me for years. And it took him a second, but he got into it. His arms wrapped round my back, his hands against my spine, sliding slowly down to my ass, which he gripped with his rough palms.

I finished opening his jeans and shoved them down over his hips, pulling him back against me so I could feel the length of his dick on my skin, hot and hard. He hissed at the contact, and I pushed myself harder into him, stroking him with my skin.

He took about a minute of it before he stepped back and shucked his pants.

Whatever I'd imagined his body would be like, the

reality was a thousand times more compelling. I brushed my hands over the thick muscles of his stomach and chest, and I imagined, all of a sudden, painting him. Not on a canvas, but with my airbrush. I imagined turning him into a Roman statue. Or a superhero. I could put a suit of armor over his naked skin and he would be beautiful.

A work of art.

It had been months since I'd thought of painting, since I'd been inspired, but Tommy in all his glory was suddenly lighting me up again.

He knocked my hand away like I was a distraction, and instead he cupped my breasts, slid his hands around my stomach, connected, with his finger, the freckles on my hip.

I got down from my knees, sitting on my ass on the bed, my legs around his, his cock, the flushed tip of it, just below my mouth. I looked up at him, just to see his face, just to see him watching me.

And he was, his ears practically on fire, and it was as hot and sweet and sexy as I always imagined it to be.

This is good-bye, I reminded myself, and I bent, licking his cock in one long sweep of my tongue. Again I did it and then slipped him inside my mouth. I just held him there for a moment, because I wanted both of us to remember this. How it felt with his cock in my mouth. Because this wouldn't happen again.

But then he pushed his fingers into my hair, cupping my skull in his fingers, pulling my hair with his calluses. He arched into me and away, and we found a slow, steady rhythm that had him panting.

That had me drenched.

I was gasping around his cock, my fingers clawing into the skin of his hips. His ass.

He pulled back suddenly. I leaned forward as if to chase him down, but he pushed me back onto the bed. I was spread out before him, my hair half across the white sheets, half trapped under my body.

He pulled off my underwear, nearly ripping it, and I kicked it off the rest of the way. Tommy's hand slid down between my legs and he stroked me with his thick fingers and soon we were both wet. So wet.

"I don't…" He shook his head like he'd forgotten what he was going to say. "Not slow."

"Okay," I agreed and pulled him down over my body. His naked skin on my naked skin was a feeling like none other. Like velvet and heat and comfort with just a little pain. My lungs couldn't pull in a full breath and my heart was beating too hard, but I opened my legs and cradled him with my body.

His cock, the incendiary heat of it, fell between my legs, into the wet of my pussy. We both gasped, and I arched my hips, rocking back and forth, fucking him a little without actually fucking him.

I slid forward and he groaned. I slid back and he groaned again. It was a slow grind against him, a tiny shift, and we were so ready, so hot for each other that it was enough.

"Get a condom," I said, and he pulled back, grabbing the box at the bedside table. He tore off the top in one big piece of cardboard, and I smiled.

"Caveman," I said.

"Stupid box," he said. He pulled out the long silver strip of condoms, and I was relieved he'd gotten a box.

This good-bye of ours might take a few tries.

The silver packet was tiny in his massive hands, and he tore the corner with his teeth, pulling out the condom. With his hands shaking he started to put it on.

"That's inside out," I told him.

He looked up, blinking. I reached out, inverted the condom and slid it over him down to the base of his cock.

I was so fond of his bemused, blank face I could barely stand it. All the remainders of our affection, of our past, of my not ever, not even a little bit resolved feelings, they all appeared, and I imagined them like tentacles reaching around him, tying us together.

"Come here," I said and scooted back on the bed. He came up over me, his knees pushing aside my knees, his hands braced beside my head. I slipped my legs up, over his thighs, urging him down to me, closer to me.

Into me.

But he stopped, held himself suspended, his face bent so I couldn't see his eyes.

"Tommy?"

He grunted and eased into the cradle of my legs, not inside me, but closer. And he stilled again.

"Please, Tommy," I breathed, arching into him, bathing him with my heat and wet and desire. He groaned and used his hand between us, notching himself against me, the head of his cock filling the entrance to my body. And again he stopped.

I reached up, lifting his head to face me. His eyes met mine, and whatever was happening, it was big. And I wondered, for one horrible, heart-stopping moment, if what nearly happened to me in that office had happened to him in that office.

"Do you want to stop?" I asked.

"God...no," he said with a huffing, hasty laugh.

He leaned down and kissed me. He kissed me and kissed me, and all my thoughts scattered. All my fears vanished. His tongue in my mouth, mine in his. The rake of his teeth.

The beautiful perfect taste of him.

"I'm a virgin," he said against my lips.

I stilled.

"What?"

"You heard me."

A thousand questions. Literally a thousand. I pushed against his shoulders, a weak attempt to get distance so I could process what the fuck he'd just said, but in that moment, he slid, hot and heavy, inside of me and I was pinned on the bed.

I gasped, stuffed full of him. I remembered worrying in the art room that he would be too big. And he almost was. He was just this side of too big.

And he was a virgin?

He was smiling, and when he pulled out and thrust back in, he was laughing. Just once. A hard bark of disbelieving joy.

I stroked his face, loving him more in this moment, with him inside my body, with his truth ringing in my ears, than I'd ever dreamed possible. And while I watched, his face sobered like he knew what I was thinking, like he saw the feelings he'd broken free when he fucked me.

"It's okay," I said, wanting to tell him that my feelings were mine and not his. This was still good-bye. "Fuck me, Tommy."

He grabbed my hands and held them above my head, and I arched against the tension. Tommy's control was broken; I could see it hanging in tatters around him. Like chains he'd broken clear through.

"Do it," I breathed.

And he pounded into me, filling me harder and fuller until I couldn't breathe. I couldn't move; I lay there and took it. I pushed against his hand, and when he didn't let go, I said, "I want to come. Let me go or use your finger—"

He held my wrists with one hand and put his other hand between my legs, his fingers pushing down and against my clit, and I immediately fell apart, the orgasm tearing me to pieces.

"Again," he said. "I want you to come again."

I nodded, because I could. I would. And his thumb rode my clit and his cock rode me and his arms held me down and I came again and just as the wave rolled over me, he stopped. And he watched.

Good-bye, I thought. And fell apart.

And then he did the same, jerking into me and coming with a hoarse shout that sounded like surprise. But I wouldn't know. Because I kept my eyes closed. Unable to watch.

20

Beth

I WOKE UP to the empty bed and a cleaned-out cottage. The front door was open, letting in a big bright sheet of sunlight and morning air that smelled like pine needles. At the bottom of the bed, Pest barked.

On the bedside table there were three torn condom wrappers.

Good-bye took three times, and I still wasn't sure it had stuck.

We didn't talk. We didn't say one word, about today or his being a virgin. Or why. We fell into a restless sleep as soon as he rolled off me that first time, and I woke up to him rolling me onto my stomach, his fingers between my legs, an orgasm roaring through me before I was fully coherent.

Hours later, as dawn lit the room in shades of pink and gray, I woke him up with my hand on his dick, and then my mouth.

Three good-byes and I felt worse than ever.

Pest jumped up on the bed, running in circles around my body.

"I'm up," I muttered and sat up, pushing back my hair. I was naked. And at this point I wasn't sure if I had any clothes left. But then I saw the stack of clothes on the chair. New sweatpants. The wolf shirt. Another pair of underwear from the three pack he'd bought me.

Tommy came in as I was pulling the shirt over my head.

"I've checked us out," he said.

"How much do I owe you?" I asked, feeling painfully awkward. *I took your virginity last night.* Honestly, that was all I could think, like we were in high school again. I wanted to talk about it. I had, without exaggeration, a million questions. All of them I knew I couldn't ask, because he would never answer them. "I mean, we should split the cost—"

"I'm not splitting it with you," he said and went over to the stash of food, throwing what couldn't be taken with us into the garbage.

The oranges hit the metal can with a *thunk.*

"Well, for a kidnapping I have to say the accommodations have been top-notch." I aimed for a joke.

"I try," he said, throwing away the carrots and the Doritos I'd brought him.

"You know I'm joking," I said. "I think… you

didn't kidnap me as much as save me. Again."

He smiled at me over his shoulder, a tight-lipped thing that spoke of feelings far more complicated than joy. I remembered, all at once, forcing his face into a smile in the art room.

You were a virgin! I thought, wanting to scream it! Wanting to discuss it. Wanting to force him into answering my questions. *How is that possible?*

But he looked away, and I pulled on the clean underwear and the sweatpants.

"Have you figured out where you want to go?" he asked. "Where you want me to drop you? Back in Santa Barbara?"

"That's not my house. The label rented it for me. I live in a one-bedroom apartment off Le Brea in Los Angeles."

"That's where you want to go?"

I nodded. "I need to mend some bridges and start working on some new songs. I leave for Europe in a few months. I have some asses to kiss."

"Sounds exciting," he said like he was a stranger, and I smiled at him like I was a stranger. Like he was a reporter in some stupid press junket.

And not the man whose virginity I took last night.

"It is."

He took Pest out to the car, and I brushed my teeth, put on a thick coat of red lipstick and some winged eyeliner, braided my hair and put it up in a genie knot on the top of my head. And within twenty minutes we were pulling away from the cottage.

Pest was standing in my lap, her paws on the window, watching the cabin behind us. I rubbed my hands through Pest's fur, happy to have someone to touch.

"Thank you, Yucca Family Lodge," I said. "You were good to us."

Tommy was silent as we pulled out of the compound.

"Where are we?" I asked. "I mean...I don't even know what state we're in."

"Western edge of Arizona," he said. "We'll be in California in about an hour."

I nodded like that suited me just fine. "Where are you going to go?" I asked. I looked at him for as long as I could, until all the things we weren't saying got to be too painful, and then I looked back out the window. "Back to the city?"

He blew out a deep breath. "Not...right away."

"Because of Bates? Because you didn't pay the debt?" I felt responsible for that...sort of. This whole thing was twisted around us so hard I wasn't sure what was whose fault.

"It's probably not safe there."

Not now. Maybe not ever.

"What do you think he'll do?" I asked.

He shrugged.

"Will he hurt you?"

"You don't need to worry—"

"Well, I am, so maybe do the right thing and talk to me about it."

He blew out a breath. "I don't think he'll hurt me," he said.

"But you don't know for sure?"

"I don't. But all the threats of what would happen to me if I didn't pay the debt had to do with having another crime pinned on me."

"And Carissa was going to cut off your balls if you touched me."

"I suppose I need to worry about that too," he said with a wry smile.

"Oh my God," I breathed.

"Beth," he said quietly, "I made the choice not to drop you off with your mother. I touched you... I knew the consequences, and I still did it. None of this is your fault."

It felt, remarkably, like it was my fault.

"What about your mother?" he asked. "Will she be looking for you?"

"Oh, she'll have something up her sleeve. She always does."

"Are you sure it's safe for you in Los Angeles?"

"She won't hurt me," I said with perhaps more

conviction than I really felt. "I'm not a kid anymore. But all your stuff in San Francisco. Your whole life. You just…leave it behind?"

He glanced at me and then away, his gaze searing for just that second.

"Don't worry about it," he said, and his dismissal stung.

"Oh, okay. I just… won't worry about it. I will in fact completely forget you once you drop me off. Tommy who?"

"That was the deal, Beth."

"Yeah, that was the deal before I knew you were a virgin, Tommy!"

Pest whined, looking between us like we were scaring her.

"Sorry, Pest," I breathed, stroking her crazy fur.

"I don't think that fact changes anything," he said quietly.

"Maybe not for you, but I fucking deflowered you."

He smiled at me, but I refused to let this go. "Yes, you did," he said. "You fucking deflowered me."

"I'm not laughing."

"I see that."

"Why?" I asked.

"Why what?"

"Why were you not having sex? A guy like you… you could have been fucking anyone you wanted."

"So Simon was fond of telling me."

"Did something… Was it the Pastor?"

His face sharpened.

"When you got taken to the office," I said in a shaky voice. "Did he—"

Tommy shook his head. "Rape me. No."

"It's been seven years, Tommy."

"I realize that."

"There was never another girl? Or boy?"

"No boy or girl," he said.

"Then why?"

"I think," he said, hitting the blinker to exit the highway. "We need coffee. And gas."

"You can't avoid this conversation forever," I said.

He pulled into a parking spot and turned to me, his arm stretched out across the back of the seat. So close he could touch me if he wanted.

But he didn't.

"I only have to avoid it for about five more hours, until I drop you back in Los Angeles, Beth. I'm not talking about the last seven years. It's over and I think…for the first time in my life, I'm ready to move on from everything that happened there. I'm leaving the ghosts where they are."

"But—"

"You and I are not meant to be together. Not now. Not seven years ago."

I exhaled slowly. I mean, we'd been talking about good-bye, but this felt... real now. He didn't want me. And I didn't want him...not in any real long-term way, I mean; it wouldn't work. I had a life to repair, a reputation to rebuild. A metric shit ton of work to do. I had no time for being with Tommy. I knew without having to experience it that it would suck me in. Suck me up.

So, he was right. We didn't belong together.

But I still wanted him to want me.

I wanted him to feel shitty that it wouldn't work. Not happy.

"You want to stop and eat here?" I asked in a slow voice. The gas station was attached to a big family-style restaurant, and we hadn't eaten real food in some time. Him especially. And now that I'd fucked him, I wanted to watch him eat, eat until he was full.

Another thing I'd wished for when we were kids.

"Grab some stuff to go," he said and handed me cash. "I'll gas up and go to the bathroom. I'll meet you back here."

I nodded, feeling numb. Right. Of course. He needed to drop me off.

We needed to be done with each other.

I wanted to weep. But I didn't. Because I had a job to do, and that was to get some coffees to go, maybe a breakfast sandwich or three, and then I had to get the hell out of Tommy's life.

I got out of the truck and walked across the puddle-splashed parking area. Jumping over and weaving around puddles.

A bell rang out as I stepped into the family restaurant and I was literally assaulted by sound. People talking. TV's. There were gaming machines in the corner blinking and chiming. I wanted to put my hands over my ears. Tommy and I had been in a tiny silent bubble for three days and I'd gotten used to it.

The real world was loud.

And abrasive. Even the smell of bacon and coffee and fried potatoes in the air—which I loved—almost seemed like too much.

And one of the real perks of my career being in disguise was that I could go out in public without people being all over me, but it felt walking through the crowded restaurant, like people were staring at me.

It's the hair, I thought.

But when I passed a man in a trucker cap who quickly tapped the shoulder of the woman next to him and tried—with zero skill—to not point at me while totally pointing at me, I started to wonder if it wasn't just the hair.

TV's lined the dining room, and I passed one with the sound turned up. The picture changed and I stopped in my tracks.

It was my mother on the screen.

"My daughter, Beth Renshaw, known better as her stage name Jada," she was saying in that voice… that fucking voice that meant people would be doing what she wanted because she expected it, "is in danger. From herself and from the man that kidnapped her from the drug rehab facility where she was to undergo rehabilitation for opiates and get psychiatric counseling."

And then it wasn't my mother on the screen with her perfect suit and her do-as-I-say voice. It was a picture of me taken when I was out at McDonald's just the other day. Like… yesterday. I gasped. Walked backward.

The picture changed and the next one was Tommy and he had a pair of emoticon socks in his hand.

Bile rose up in my throat. My mother was having me followed. My mother…

I turned and, trying really hard not to make a scene, walked back to the front door. But at the gas bays, Tommy wasn't standing by the truck.

Tommy

I WATCHED BETH jump over a silver rain puddle on her way into the family restaurant just as the meter clicked to a stop and I put the gas nozzle back. The smell of gasoline and a recent rain filled the cool air.

She was pissed, I was pretty sure. Pissed that I wouldn't answer her questions about why I'd still been a virgin. Mostly I was embarrassed to talk about it. Who confessed those kinds of things? And a little bit I was scared to talk about it, which didn't make a lot of sense, but this feeling sat in the back of my brain, warning me not to get into this with her.

I was scared that talking about it would make it real, make what we'd done some kind of tangible tie between us—and it was, of course it was—but I needed it to stay indescribable.

Beth wanted to talk and frame out the parameters of everything. She wanted every thought and feeling to be turned into something concrete. It's what she'd been asking for in the cabin. To name all our ghosts. Pin down all our demons.

But I didn't know how to do that and keep on living.

Because it was going to be hard enough to walk away from her.

I kicked open the door to the men's room that was on the outside of the gas station, and couldn't get too worked up about the the disgusting condition of the place.

That was the sex talking, I imagined. Even terrible things didn't seem so bad with this easy boneless feeling I had going in my body.

I hoped the women's room was better, for Beth's sake.

Jada, I reminded myself and then realized it didn't matter. It was over.

We don't belong together. We didn't seven years ago. And we don't now.

And it didn't hurt. Not in the sharp way I'd grown used to. But it ached. And it would ache, I guessed, for the rest of my life.

The wall of urinals was on the far side of the bathroom. Two stalls on the side near the door. The door closed behind me, and the bathroom became a dark cave. I picked the far urinal and unzipped.

The door opened behind me, and I finished peeing, zipped back up and turned, only to find two men standing in front of the door, their arms crossed over their chests.

The door closed behind them, making the room dark, and one of them reached over and flipped on the light.

They were still looking at me.

"Morning," I said, my skin tightening over my body, and I walked over to the sink, watching the men in the mirror as I turned on the faucet to wash my hands.

The guys weren't here to use the bathroom. They

were here for me.

"You Tommy MacNeill?" one of the guys asked.

"Who wants to know?" I scanned the room for some kind of weapon. There was a mop bucket in the corner, with the mop in it. The paper towel dispenser looked like it would come off the wall without any effort. I edged sideways, closer to the mop. I'd break the handle over my leg, and I'd be able to do some damage.

The other man, a thin Filipino guy, took out some black gloves and started putting them on. He smiled like he was really looking forward to trying to beat the shit out of me.

"My name's Sammy," he said. "And I got a message for you from Mr. Bates."

A NOTE FROM MOLLY

Hi, guys! I hope you enjoyed LOST WITHOUT YOU!

If you're ready for more of Tommy and Beth (and everyone else from St. Joke's):
WHERE I BELONG

If you'd like up-to-date information on new releases, please join my newsletter list
www.molly-okeefe.com/subscribe
or follow me on Bookbub:
bookbub.com/authors/molly-o-keefe

And for lots of fun giveaways, freebies, takeovers and book chats, join my Facebook group:
facebook.com/groups/1657059327869189

And please drop me a line anytime
molly@molly-okeefe.com

Please consider leaving a review for Lost Without You. Reviews—good or bad—help readers find books!

Thanks again!!

Made in the USA
Columbia, SC
15 September 2017